I0678440

E.J. RUSSELL

DEATH ON DENIAL

QUEST INVESTIGATIONS
BOOK FOUR

Cover art: L.C. Chase, http://lcchase.com
Edited by Meg DesCamp

ISBN: 978-1-947033-39-9

First edition
March 2022

Contact information:
ejr@ejrussell.com

E.J. RUSSELL

DEATH ON DENIAL

QUEST INVESTIGATIONS
BOOK FOUR

For Dame Agatha Christie, with apologies for the pun.

CHAPTER ONE

"You want me to do *what*?" I goggled at my boyfriend, whose resting grump face was softened by a hopeful half-smile.

"Go on a wee swim with me." Lachlan held up a bundle of glossy, short brown fur the same color as the darker streaks in his hair. "In my skin." He ducked his chin, pink infusing his tanned cheeks. "You've never seen me in my skin."

And *that*, my friends, was the problem. I *wanted* to see him in his skin, every six-foot-six, broad-shouldered, beefcake-gorgeous inch of it. But he wasn't talking about *that* skin. Nope, he was talking about his *seal* skin. As in, sometimes he's a seal—and not the Navy kind. Nope, an actual seal.

Yeah, my boyfriend. The selkie. Not only a selkie, but the selkie *king*, if he'd ever bother to take the throne.

And me? Just a human ex-tabloid photographer who somehow got lucky enough to earn a place with the supernatural community, land a job with Quest Investigations, and score a super- hot boyfriend who sometimes had flippers instead of hands and feet. #lifegoals.

"I've already seen you in your seal skin," I grumbled as I braced myself against the rocking of *Cridhe na Mara*, Lachlan's cabin cruiser, "so that argument won't fly."

His eyebrow, the one bisected with the thin white scar, shot up. "You have? When?"

"During our first case." It was my turn to blush. "I kind of watched you when you went over the side after we found that dead herring in your berth."

Lachlan grinned, altogether too smug. "See anything you like?"

"Don't be a jerk. You know I did." My eyes widened. "You, um, replaced that mattress, right?"

His grin faded, and he laid his seal skin across the pilot's chair so he could rest his hands on my shoulders. "Of course I did. Your comfort is everything to me, Matthew." He nudged my chin up and kissed me softly. "If I have my way, you'll never be anything but comfortable, happy, and contented."

I peered up at him, smiling slyly. "I'd be *very* comfortable, happy, and contented if you took me to bed right now." What can I say? I've got zero game.

"I want you to understand me. To know me. This"—he gestured to the ocean and to his seal skin—"is who I am. It's a part of me."

"You know what's a part of me?" I said testily. "The part that objects to voluntary hypothermia."

"Matthew." My shiver wasn't entirely the result of the throaty burr in Lachlan's voice when he said my name, because the wind off the water was freaking *cold*, even in the shelter of the pilothouse. "I need you to embrace *all* of me."

I hugged my jacket tighter to my chest. "I'd prefer to embrace all of you in front of a nice, cozy fire. Or better yet, in a nice cozy bed."

Lachlan chuckled and stroked my face. "We'll get there. I promise. And the sooner you're in the sea, the sooner I'll be able to keep you warm."

I leaned into his touch and sighed. *Just remember that berth waiting for us down below.* "Fine. Let's get this over with."

His smile nearly melted my bones, and if I got a little distracted watching him take off his clothes, baring every inch—and there were a *lot* of inches, if you get my drift—of his skin?

Trust me, if you could have seen him, you'd have been drooling too. If I wasn't so obsessed with all things supernatural, I'd have almost objected when he pulled on his seal skin. Except he bent over to slip it over his feet, so you know, there was *that*. I might have whimpered.

He heard me, because of course he did, and paused with the skin pulled up to his waist. "Matthew?

"Right. Sorry." I glanced around the pilothouse. "Where's my wetsuit? Is it below?"

His brows drew together in confusion. "There's no wetsuit."

"A dry suit then?" That would be better. I'd heard that wetsuits weren't exactly toasty.

"Matthew." He approached me again, his lower half encased in that fur that looked softer than silk and fit him like, well, a second skin. He still had the usual number of legs and feet—he couldn't shift unless he was actually in the ocean—and his chest was bare and dusted with *another* kind of fur. *Rawr*. "I thought you understood. All your skin must be touched by the sea, as is mine."

My jaw sagged. "Are you *serious* right now? You want me to go in the water *naked*?" My ears heated, a sure sign my anger was about to get the better of me. "It's *November*, Lachlan." I pointed over the stern, where the Oregon coast was still visible across what now seemed a vast expanse of choppy waves. "And that's the freaking *Pacific Ocean*."

"Aye." His tone implied that this was all completely reasonable. Which, in case you haven't gotten the memo, it was not.

I scrubbed my hands over my face, my fingers catching in my beard, which could probably use a trim. "Lachlan. This day has already been hell. Literally."

He frowned. "What do you mean?"

"I mean that before I showed up at the marina to meet you, I spent the morning in Sheol—"

"You went to Sheol?" His frown morphed into a full-on glower. "Why?"

"I was at a photoshoot with Paimon."

"That demon who wanted you to update his headshots?"

"If only headshots were all he wanted," I muttered.

Lachlan actually growled. "Did that wanker put his hands on you?"

"Down, boy. No. But he decided he wanted some swimsuit shots. Next to the lava river, because, and I quote, *It makes my eyes pop.*" I shuddered. My eyes were the ones doing the popping, because Paimon had more than the usual number of appendages barely contained in his tiny speedo. He claimed the extra equipment saved on refraction time. Which, you know, good for Paimon, assuming his partners were on board and had given full, non-coerced consent, but whatever.

My problem was I still hadn't encountered *Lachlan's* appendage. We'd had a number of *extremely* hot make-out sessions, but every time we started to take it further, we got interrupted. If it wasn't a call from my office—and Quest had been inundated with a rash of minor theft cases lately—it was one of Lachlan's regular fishing tour bookings, or another of his visits to support our friend Blair as they got settled in Faerie.

Now, I don't begrudge Lachlan's time with Blair. I mean, Blair was doing great, considering they'd just relocated to a home in another freaking *dimension*, but it was definitely a lot, and Lachlan was their only link to the life they'd always known. And I certainly couldn't fault him for attending to his job, since my workload in the last few weeks had been the cockblocking culprit just as often.

But I'd been certain when he invited me on this private outing on his boat that we'd finally have the chance for some mutual naked exploration in the berth—with its brand new mattress, thank you, Lachlan.

I'd never dreamed that our first skin-to-skin encounter would be under the freaking Pacific. The instant I put a toe in that water, my junk would retreat so far inside my body I'd need to go spelunking to find it.

Not the best first impression to lay on a new lover.

I tried another tactic. "But there could be sharks. Great whites. You said so yourself."

Lachlan chuckled. "Aye, sharks live in these waters, but they won't come near us." He cradled my face in his hands. "Selkies may look like seals, but inside, we're still supes. We've our own protections, our own magic, to keep the beasties at bay. You'll be safe with me. Always."

Drat. There went that argument. "What if someone sees me?" We were beyond the jetty, anchored in the open ocean, but with land still in sight.... I really didn't want to be flashing my fish-belly white butt to somebody with a high-powered telescope—or worse, a drone camera. Hell, a few years ago, if I'd had a hint that something like Lachlan's shift was about to happen, *I'd* have been the one with the long-distance recording equipment.

"No one will see you, *mo cridhe*. No one but me."

Okay, game over. My Gaelic was minimal at best, but I knew what he'd just called me. *My heart*. There might be someone in the universe with the willpower to resist Lachlan Brodie after that, especially when his eyes crinkled at the corners with his soft smile, but that someone was not me.

"The heat's already on down below?"

"Aye."

"There's towels?"

"On the locker by the transom, ready and waiting."

"Coffee?"

"In the galley."

"The berth's got plenty of blankets?"

"Oh, aye." He waggled his eyebrows. "But you won't be needing those, not with me to warm you."

I blinked, suddenly dizzy as my blood rushed south. "Let's go."

He chuckled again as he slipped his arms into the skin—which isn't as creepy as it sounds. His seal skin looks more like a super-deluxe wetsuit than a deboned seal. "Trust me, *mo cridhe*, you can't be any keener than I am to have you in my bed at last."

If that was the case, then I didn't know why we had to endure virtual cryo-immersion first, but...*mo cridhe*? Nope. No way could I turn him down now.

I shrugged out of my jacket. *Brrrr.* "So how does this work, exactly?"

"I'll go in first and shift. Then you slip over the transom, easy as you please, and get on my back."

The transom was at least close to the water, so I didn't have to negotiate a ladder. The sea wasn't especially rough today—it was cloudy, normal for Oregon at this time of year, but not stormy—but it was still the ocean, so, you know, not exactly motionless. "On your back?" At least my front would be warm. Ish.

"Aye. Put your arms around my neck." His gaze was hot, intent, and I'd never heard Lachlan *breathless* before. "And we'll swim. Together."

"Okay." I tried to put a little more confidence in my voice. "Right. Let's do this."

He kissed me, soft and slow. "Thank you, *mo cridhe*. You have made me the happiest of men."

The seal fur didn't give me anything to grab onto, so I laced my fingers behind his neck. "You're *sure* we can't skip the naked swim and go straight to bed?"

"I'm sure." He kissed me again, far too quickly for my liking, and strode across the deck and down the starboard stairs to the low transom. He slipped into the water without a splash, and between one blink and the next...well, he was a seal, gazing up at me as he bobbed gently in the waves.

"The things I do for love," I muttered.

I figured this was one of those rip-the-Band-Aid-off situations and stripped quickly. "Holy crap, Lachlan," I said as I hurried down the six steps from the deck to the transom, "it's freaking *freezing* out here." I was essentially made of gooseflesh, and my junk was already retreating in terror, but...*mo cridhe*. I could do this.

The waves slapping against the stern sent spray over my bare legs. *Yikes!* I glared at the seal. "If I squeal like a little kid when I jump in, you are *not* allowed to hold it over my head in the future." Since seals always look like they're smiling anyway, I couldn't tell whether Lachlan was amused or just waiting for me to get on with it.

Rather than leaping in, I squatted on the edge of the transom and sort of pushed myself over the edge in a fetal position.

Uuunnnngh. My breath halted, frozen in my chest as all my muscles rebelled at the outrage. A sharp ache started in my fingers and toes and started to creep up my arms and legs. *Breathe, Matt, breathe.* I managed one gasp. Two. Three. I wasn't sure where I'd find a fourth, but then something smooth and warm brushed against my side, and a seal—*Lachlan*—was there, peering at me out of enormous liquid brown eyes. He nudged me with his muzzle, repeatedly, insistently.

Oh. Right. I was supposed to get on his back. Since my arms were clutched against my chest in a vain attempt to keep my core warm, and felt about as mobile as a couple of icicles, I wasn't sure how I'd manage that. Teeth chattering, I *willed* myself to unclutch and reach for Lachlan's sturdy neck. *Just another inch. One more. One—*

"Hey, Hugh!"

This was it. I was clearly experiencing hypothermia-induced hallucinations, because there was no way *Jordan*, Quest's werewolf intern, could possibly be grinning down at me sunnily from the deck, with Frang, my usual Fae Transportation Association driver, looming behind him.

Jordan's brow puckered. "Kind of cold for a swim, isn't it? Oh, hey. Is that Lachlan? Hi, Lachlan!"

Apparently seals can roll their eyes. Or maybe that was a selkie thing. If Lachlan could see him too, that must mean I wasn't imagining this. "J-J-Jordan? What are you doing here?" I didn't have to ask how he'd gotten here—Frang's presence explained that. He'd obviously escorted Jordan through Faerie and into the middle of the freaking ocean. "Wh-wh-where's Doop?" Jordan never went anywhere without his attendant hellhound these days.

"He's staying at the Dog House with the other guys today. We're working on separation anxiety."

"His or yours?"

"Um…" He screwed up his face. "Both? But it was a good thing, since Doop freaks Frang out and I needed his help today."

Lachlan bumped up against me, smooth and blessedly warm. I managed to sling one numb arm over his neck. "Help for what?"

"To get here, of course." He glanced over his shoulder. "There's, um, some people who want to see you."

"See me?" I didn't want anybody to see me right now, including Jordan and Frang, and *especially* Lachlan, since I probably resembled a flash-frozen maggot.

"Well, not *only* you. They're here for Lachlan, too."

I didn't think I could get colder, but apparently I was wrong. "What do you mean, *here*?"

He grimaced. "Weeeellll…"

CHAPTER TWO

An alarming number of people surrounded Jordan, all of them grinning down at us—and I mean, really? Lachlan's boat was good-sized, but it wasn't a freaking ocean liner. Could it *hold* this many people safely? Plus, I'd never seen any of these people before. One of them, a tall man with tanned, creased cheeks and a shock of the whitest hair I'd ever seen, pushed to the front next to Jordan. He looked a little like Sir Ian McKellen as Gandalf the White, only burlier. I couldn't see any of them below the waist because of the aft locker, so I couldn't tell if he was wearing wizardly robes under his puffer jacket, although he held a wrist-thick wooden staff in one hand. A walking stick, maybe? Since they'd appeared out of nowhere, they must be supes, so the staff could be anything from a magic wand to fuel for a ritual bonfire. He gripped the railing with his other hand and bowed.

Next to me, Lachlan-the-seal morphed back into his human form. "Bloody hell," he muttered. "It's the selkies."

I stared at him, eyes wide. "The selkies. You mean your subjects?"

"They're not my subjects," he groused.

The rest of them bowed and selkie-Gandalf intoned, "Your Majesty."

"Not sure they've gotten that message, pal." And now I had to get out of the water in front of them. Naked.

You know, now that I thought about it? Hypothermia wasn't so bad. In fact, it was looking better by the minute.

"I'd best see what they want. Otherwise we'll never be shed of them." Lachlan braced his palms on the transom and just sort of *flowed* out of the water and onto the boat.

I doubted my exit would be quite as graceful, since A) I lacked his musculature, B) I wasn't a magical sea creature, and C) I wasn't entirely sure my body hadn't completely solidified.

Lachlan turned to look down at me, a rueful smile on his lips, and held out his hands. "Come, *mo cridhe*. Our first swim will have to wait, but it will happen, make no mistake."

"Somehow, I d-d-don't find that particularly reassuring." I tried to reach up to him, but my arms had other ideas and refused to leave the marginal shelter of my chest.

"Ah, shite." He dropped to one knee, plunged his hands in the water, and hooked them under my arms. Then—I kid you not—he deadlifted me onto the boat along with a wash of sea water, and held me against his seal-furred chest, blocking me from the peanut gallery's view. "I'm sorry. This is not how I wished our day to go."

"You and me both," I muttered, as feeling began to return to my extremities.

"Hey, guys," Jordan called. "Want some towels? And your clothes?" I peered over Lachlan's shoulder in time to see the towels—and what looked suspiciously like my boxer briefs—slip from Jordan's hands and tumble to the transom. Directly into the water that had just accompanied me out of the sea.

"Sorry!" Jordan set the rest of my clothes on the locker with exaggerated care. "I'll go find more towels." He vanished from the railing, but the rest of the crowd remained, looking far too interested in the show. At least none of them had come down the stairs to get a closer look.

"Do you know what the selkies are doing here, Lachlan?" I murmured.

He scowled—Lachlan is a world-class scowler, which I shouldn't find as hot as I did, considering my last unrequited crush was on a man who never stopped smiling. "Sticking their flippers where they don't belong. Sodding nosy parkers."

I'd started shivering like a Jell-O mold, which I suppose was good, since it meant my body hadn't completely shut down. As Lachlan showed no sign of wanting to join his uninvited guests, I burrowed against his chest. He assisted by wrapping his arms around me, and wow. He was better than an electric blanket. I peered up into his face. "Why would they show up here?"

His scowl turned into a sheepish grimace. "Because I wouldn't go there?"

I narrowed my eyes. "Go where, exactly?"

He signed. "To the clan muster."

"I'm guessing they invited you." My tone was the only dry thing about me at the moment.

"Oh, aye. More times than I can count."

"Have they ever—" I eyed the crowd on the deck, who were all still staring at the two of us avidly and with far more satisfaction than seemed warranted. Scratch that—Lachlan was *always* a satisfying vista, but given the sizes and shapes of the selkie brigade, I didn't think sightings of buff folks in seal skins were all that rare. "Have they ever stalked you like this before?"

"Not in person." He glanced over his shoulder, the scowl back in force.

"Then why now?"

"I told you. They're sodding nosy parkers."

"But—"

"Got 'em!" Jordan called from behind the selkie looky-loos, towels waving in the air above their heads like semaphores. Once they jostled aside to let him pass—not easy, considering they were packed more tightly than sardines—he hurtled down the stairs to present the towels to us with his habitual sunny smile. "Do you want me to bring your clothes down too, Hugh?"

"N-n-no, thanks." I snatched one of the towels and wrapped it around my waist as Lachlan draped another one over my shoulders. No way was I getting dressed down here in full view of the selkies *and* Jordan. Besides, pulling my jeans on with my legs still damp would result in an extremely ungraceful reverse strip tease. "I'll get a little dryer first." I thought longingly of the berth below deck, with its blankets and attendant space heater, but I didn't want to walk through the crowd in nothing but a towel. True, it was a Lachlan-sized bath sheet, but togas had never been a good look on me.

Lachlan must have picked up on my uneasiness, because he dropped a kiss on my hair. "I'll get rid of them, *mo cridhe.*" When he draped a third towel over my head, I probably resembled the third shepherd in a low-rent Nativity play. "Take shelter in the pilothouse as soon as I take them below."

Jordan bit his lip, scanning the people clustered on deck above us. "I know your boat is a decent size, Lachlan, but there's a lot of selkies. Will they all fit down there?" He pointed at Frang, towering a head over the tallest of the selkies, who was at least Lachlan's size. "I mean, I know Frang won't. He can't get past the hatch." He leaned in and whispered, "Besides, I think the rocking of the boat is getting to him. Doesn't he look a little green to you?"

I glanced up at Frang. "How can you tell?" As a duergar, a sort of meta-troll, Frang's skin always looked a little greenish-brown to me, kind of like lichen on a boulder. I glanced back at Jordan, who didn't even sway when a swell rocked the boat. "And furthermore, why aren't *you* seasick? I thought you hated the water."

Jordan shrugged. "Me and Doop have been practicing with Gage, a coastal werewolf who's part of the Dog House pack." He wrinkled his nose. "He took us *fishing*. Twice. His birth pack runs an ocean excursion business out of their Lincoln County base. Kind of like yours, Lachlan, only there's more boats."

Lachlan kissed me again, on the lips this time, although all too briefly. "I'll be as quick as I can." He took the starboard stairs two at a time. The muscles bunching in his legs and butt were perfectly outlined by his seal skin.

"Wow," Jordan breathed.

I frowned at him, but by his expression, he wasn't ogling Lachlan with the same libidinous thoughts as I was. "What?"

"I've never seen a selkie shift before. It's different than it is with weres. I mean, we have to take our clothes *off*, not put something *on*. I think that's how it works with most shifters. All except selkies."

I hadn't thought anything could take my mind off my near-iceberg experience or my humiliation at appearing before Lachlan's clan in nothing but gooseflesh, but new facts about the supernatural community did the trick. I huddled against the bulkhead between the staircases. "Does it hurt? Shifting, I mean?"

Jordan shook his head. "Nope. It's part of our magic." He grinned. "I mean, if it hurt, you'd never get anybody to do it, right?"

"Not necessarily," I said, thinking about the ongoing pain of my constantly interrupted intimacies with Lachlan. "Not if the result gives you a real benefit." *Like love.*

"I guess," he replied, uncertainty clear in his tone. "Luckily, we don't have to deal with it. Quentin told me that when Ted shifts—" He winced. "Sorry. I didn't mean to mention them."

The heat rushing up my neck only made me more aware of how cold I was everywhere else. Did everybody in the supe community know about my infatuation with grizzly shifter Ted Farnsworth before he married his incubus husband, Quentin Bertrand-Harrington? Probably, considering I'd confessed as much while under a truth spell in open court. Jordan hadn't been present, but one thing I'd learned about supes? They fed on gossip like it was an all-you-can-eat taco bar.

I wrapped the towel more closely around my shoulders. "It's okay, Jordan. What did Quentin tell you?"

"That when Ted shifts into his bear, there's a sound. A deep one. Like in the air."

I wished for the notebook I kept in my camera bag, the one I used to log supe information. But while I usually kept my camera close, I made an exception when I was naked in the ocean. "Does the same thing happen when werewolves shift?"

He squinted up at the clouds. "Maybe? When I'm wolfy and one of my friends shifts near me, I can always tell which one it is, even if I can't see them. I mean, they smell different, obviously, but there's something else too." He brightened. "Maybe it's like those sounds only dogs can hear, only it's werewolves instead of dogs."

I really wanted to explore this further, but not while draped in towel drag with my feet awash in sea water. The murmur of voices faded from up on deck, although I couldn't tell over the susurrus of the ocean whether Lachlan had managed to herd everyone below. Huddled against the bulkhead as I was, I couldn't see up on deck. "Have they gone?"

Jordan backed up a couple of steps and peered upward. "Everyone except Frang."

Frang I could deal with. One thing about duergars—they might prefer brawling to conversation, and downed concoctions that would fell a mammoth, but they didn't judge. "Let's go up to the pilothouse then."

As I mounted the stairs, the towel around my waist started to come loose. "Dang it." I stumbled on the last step as I tried to knot it more securely. My fingers were still figuring out how to function again, so I wasn't that successful, but it would have to do until I was dry enough to put my jeans on.

The wind was picking up as I made it onto the deck, finding its way under my towel ensemble. The swells were increasing, rocking the boat so I had to brace my feet farther apart to steady myself. "Morning, Frang."

The duergar didn't answer, simply swallowed convulsively. Apparently Jordan wasn't wrong about Frang's incipient seasickness. Weird. He could drink dragon piss muddled with holly berries, but he couldn't handle slightly rough seas. I wondered if there was a supe equivalent for Dramamine. If not, I made a mental note to ask Bryce, my boss's druid husband, whether he could whip up something.

On the other hand, having random tour groups show up on Lachlan's boat unannounced wasn't something I wanted to encourage. Instead, maybe I'd ask Bryce if it was possible to block the boat's access from Faerie. One way or another, I was determined to have privacy when Lachlan and I *finally* got past first base.

"Frang?" I didn't get too close, because if a guy that big decided to spew, he'd cover a lot of real estate. "You want to sit down?"

He shook his head frantically, which was apparently the wrong thing to do because he pressed his lips together, clapped both hands over his mouth, and lurched for the railing. Jordan and I both winced at the retching that followed.

"I should have asked for a water-based driver," Jordan said unhappily.

I raised my eyebrows. "You can do that now?" The FTA spells had been enhanced to allow riders to ask for specific drivers—which is why I usually traveled with Frang—but I hadn't heard about any other upgrades. "I didn't know the King had added a species filter."

Jordan bit his lip. "He, um, didn't. Really."

"Jordan." I infused as much reproach in my tone as I could manage through chattering teeth. "Is Hector monkeying with the magic grid again?" Jordan's werewolf friend Hector was a programming whiz, combining human tech with supe magic in ways that weren't always authorized by the supe powers-that-be.

"Not much," Jordan muttered. Which meant *Yes, one hell of a lot.* "But there were just so *many* selkies that I thought having Frang along would help to keep them in line, you know?"

"Why not just bring Doop and leave Frang to his other clients?"

"I'm not an FTA driver. Doop can only find people he knows, and needs a dimensional portal for access if we don't launch from Faerie." Jordan glanced around the pilothouse. "I don't *think* there's a dimensional portal on Lachlan's boat."

I closed my eyes. "Oh, please no."

"But I should have been more considerate of Frang. I mean, not everybody can handle water."

I had to chuckle, since Jordan had been one of those people until very recently. "We should send him back to Faerie. He doesn't need to wait here, does he?" The sound of irate voices drifted up from the open hatch, so I didn't think Lachlan had wrangled the selkies successfully yet. "Who knows how long these negotiations will take? You can always use Hector's illicit app to call another driver when the selkies are ready to leave."

"I suppose." Jordan's hesitant response was punctuated by another round of retching from Frang. "Although maybe we should wait until he's, um, done first."

I winced as Frang heaved again. "Good point. I'd offer him some water, but it's all down in the galley." I gestured to my towels. "I'm not exactly dressed for stealthy reconnaissance."

"Oh, I'll get it. Be right back."

Before I could mention that the selkie confab might not welcome a werewolf eavesdropper, Jordan ducked through the hatch. I eyed Frang, whose back was still to me. I suspected this was the most privacy I could expect in the near future, so I might as well take advantage of it.

The wind whipped the towel on my head across my face as I grabbed my stack of clothes from atop the locker and scurried back into the shelter of the pilothouse. I dropped the towels from my head and shoulders onto the pilot's chair and shook out my jeans. I'd have to go commando, which wasn't my favorite, but I wasn't about to don my waterlogged boxer briefs. With another glance at Frang, who was still, er, occupied, I unknotted the towel around my waist. It came loose, only my grip on its edge keeping it from falling.

"Hugh Mann?"

"Uh..." I clutched the towel in front of my groin, staring the man who'd suddenly appeared on deck. I tried to subtly rearrange coverage so my bare butt wasn't on display. Pro tip: Never try this in a brisk ocean breeze. "Yes?"

Jordan popped out of the hatch, holding a bottle of water. "The selkies aren't done— Oh!" He spotted the man. "Sorry. I know it's crowded down there. Did I take your spot? You can go back now. I don't think the meeting's quite done yet."

"I'm not here for the meeting." He swaggered toward me. "I'm here for Hugh." He held out a hand as though to shake.

Now, I know it was stupid. Hand-shaking isn't *required* when you meet somebody, but I was a little distracted given that I was meeting this guy while I was wearing a terry loincloth, a duergar was upchucking over the rail behind me, and some very angry voices were drifting up from below. So I did it. I held out my hand.

Unfortunately, it was the one holding the towel, and it puddled around my feet just as the man's appearance changed from human-seeming to a short, pebbly-skinned, yellow-eyed, scraggly-bearded creature wearing a ragged coverall and a red beanie. Jordan sucked in a breath and dropped the water, and the bottle rolled back and forth with the rocking of the boat.

Instead of shaking, the—maybe not a man?—bared extremely sharp teeth and slapped a thick envelope into my hand. "You've been served."

CHAPTER THREE

I stared at the process server, my mouth agape, my mind nothing but white noise because *lawsuit*. A chill breeze around my nether regions goosed me out of my fugue, reminding me that I was naked in front of a stranger with extremely sharp teeth. Then I glanced helplessly between the envelope, my jeans, and my discarded towels, somehow unable to move.

"Here, Hugh," Jordan said quietly, passing me my jeans.

I clutched them in front of my groin, hands trembling, although by now I wasn't sure if I could blame it all on the cold. "Wh-what is—"

"Redcap," Jordan murmured, and stepped between me and the process server. "Who has no business here."

The redcap touched a finger to his forehead. "Done my business, now, haven't I?" He strolled out of the pilothouse, grinned at the still retching Frang, and hopped over the gunwale. I didn't hear him hit the water.

Jordan hustled after him and peered down into the waves. "He's gone."

"Gone where?" I laid the envelope on the pilot's chair and struggled into my jeans. I managed the zipper, but I could tell the button was beyond my numb fingers, so I didn't even bother. I pulled on my thermal henley, but when I tried to don my jacket, my arms got tangled in the sleeves.

"Let me." Jordan untwisted the jacket—which I'd been trying to put on upside down—and eased it over my arms. "I'm really sorry, Hugh."

"*You're* sorry?" I wrapped my arms across my chest and tucked my hands under my armpits. "Why?"

"I didn't realize he was here."

He looked so miserable, his shoulders drooping, that I snatched the envelope off the chair. "Sit."

He plopped down with none of his usual unconscious werewolf grace. "I'm sure he wasn't there when the selkies showed up at Quest, or I'd have noticed his funky smell then. I picked it up when we were in Faerie, but Faerie always has weird smells, so I figured it was either that or, you know, one of the selkies had a hygiene issue. But I should have counted. I should have made sure that the same number went into Faerie as came out of it, and I didn't."

I eyed Frang, who'd rescued the fallen water bottle and was guzzling it with a whimper. "You might not have counted, but then, it's not your job, is it?" I approached Frang, although not too closely. "Frang, how many riders did you clock entering Faerie from Quest?"

He belched, but at least didn't lunge for the rail again. "Twenty-two."

"And how many exited here on the boat?"

His fingers tightened on the water bottle in a crinkle of plastic. "Twenty-three. That'll change the fare."

I sighed. Frang was a good guy, did his job well, but wasn't a very creative thinker. From the looks of the redcap, he'd probably been Unseelie before the Convergence, the same as Frang, so Frang probably wouldn't have found the funky smell unusual. Besides, Frang's job as an FTA driver had parameters: riders and fares, period. His charge wasn't to ask *why* someone had called him, only where they wanted to go. "It's not your fault, Jordan."

"But it is! I should have paid more attention." He huddled in the chair, his hands dangling between his knees. "I should never have left Doop at the Dog House. *He'd* never have missed the smell. I'm never leaving him at home again!"

I hunkered down in front of him. "Tell me about redcaps."

Jordan blinked at me, clearly trying to change direction from his spiral into self-recrimination. "Well, they used to be Unseelie before the Convergence."

"I gathered that much," I said dryly. One of the first things I'd learned about the fae was that Seelie fae were absolutely required to be beautiful in the classical sense. Unseelie fae had a little more *leeway* when it came to physical appearance.

"My friend Tanner's studying supe history, and he says they started out as random killers. Their hats are red because"—he swallowed convulsively, and I wondered whether he needed a trip to the railing—"because they soaked them in their victim's blood." His face scrunched up. "But dried blood isn't red. It's that weird brown color, right? Wouldn't they be browncaps instead? Although I supposed that doesn't sound very scary."

"So they started out randomly murdering people. Did they eventually change?"

Jordan nodded. "Tanner says that they ended up more as assassins, since they were stealthy and their victims never saw them coming." He chuckled weakly. "He said they probably figured there was more gold in it for them if they hired themselves out rather than ambushing random travelers."

"I'm guessing the King put the kybosh on that little cottage industry when he took the throne."

"Aye," Frang rumbled. "No more killing, but they prefer to tackle the unpleasant tasks. Work that's...that's..."

I eyed the envelope as though it were about to sprout teeth as formidable as the redcap's. "Confrontational?" Frang nodded. "Where did he disappear to?"

Frang lifted his chin with as much pride as a guy with vomit dappling his homespun jerkin could manage. "Us proper FTA drivers have good jobs now. Respect, whether we were Unseelie before or not. Redcaps? Well, their tasks are as unpleasant as their stench. Who'd request us for a ride if they knew we were nothing more than getaway drivers?" His face crumpled, and I was afraid we were in for another spewfest. But instead he sniffed, the way I do when I get ambushed by a sentimental holiday commercial. "The King understood that. So he arranged for redcaps to use Faerie as transport, same as us, as long as the trip's part of their assignment."

I stood. "So redcaps are stealthy. They can enter and exit Faerie at will. And they're fulfilling a"—I glared at the envelope —"necessary but unpleasant function. I don't think there's anything either one of you could have done to keep them away from me."

"But I could have tried. I should have *known*," Jordan wailed.

"I should have counted," Frang added.

"And I should have been smart enough not to hop into the ocean naked in November, so we've all got regrets." I glanced between Frang and Jordan, making sure I had their attention. "So let's move on, shall we?" I still wasn't completely warm, but I wasn't a Popsicle either, and though my belly still roiled with apprehension when I looked at that fat envelope, ignoring it wouldn't make it go away. It was a problem I had to solve, so I needed to get down to it. "Frang, why don't you head back to Faerie, change your shirt, and take a bicarb, or whatever you need to feel better."

His lumpy brow furrowed. "But the riders down below—"

"Can call for another driver when they're ready to leave." I glanced irritably at the hatch, where the cacophony of voices hadn't abated. "They show zero signs of that at the moment, so they can take their chances." I flapped my hands at him. "Go on. Shoo."

He sighed, but when the boat rocked suddenly again, he clapped both hands over his mouth, turned, and vanished.

I picked up the envelope. "Guess I'd better see who's suing me, eh?" I turned it over in my hands. "I've been at a supe trial before, but it was a criminal case." In fact, I'd nearly been one of the defendants. "This is, I guess, a civil suit? Does Faerie have a civil service? Small claims courts? A Judge Judy equivalent?" I knew they didn't have law enforcement analogous to the human police force. They had enforcers with really big swords —my boss Mal had been one of them, and his brother Alun still was—but Quest Investigations was their only investigative arm.

Jordan's eyebrows bunched. "I think so?" He was still huddled in the pilot's chair, but at least he'd lost his woebegone expression. "I'm not an expert on Faerie, though. We'd need to ask Eleri."

I debated whether I should contact Eleri, my self-described dryad BFF, but then I remembered: There were already twenty-four people on the boat, including Lachlan and me, and I was pretty sure this vessel was never intended to hold that many. Time enough to ask her about it later. My cell phone had no service here, so I couldn't exactly call her. Although... "Jordan, does your phone still have Hector's magical signal boost?"

"Um..." His gaze shifted to a point above my left shoulder. "Yes?"

"Could you call Eleri, please, and put her on speaker?"

Jordan brightened immediately. "Sure thing, Hugh!"

He pulled his phone from his jacket pocket, hit the screen— no matter what any of us said, Jordan still didn't password-protect his phone—and barely an instant later Eleri answered.

"Hey, Jordan, what's up?"

"Hi, Eleri. You're on speaker with me and Hugh. We're on Lachlan's boat."

Her chuckle was downright evil. "Are you being punished for something, Jordan? I know you'd rather be anywhere but on the water."

Jordan huffed. "I'm fine. But Hugh has some questions for you about Faerie. Is this a good time?"

"Are you kidding?" Her tone oozed exasperation. "The dryad grove is trying to elect a new clan chief, and we've been reduced to squabbling over inconsequential nonsense for the last three hours. Please. Give me something else to think about."

Eleri's former clan chief had been uprooted permanently after his involvement in a kidnapping had been discovered in our last big case, and she'd been complaining ever since about how slowly the dryad leadership was moving to replace him. She and her "book club," a group of the more progressive dryads, were advocating for more sweeping changes than the other OG —old growth—contingent. I had faith in Eleri's ruthlessness and persistence, even if her patience was wearing thin.

"What do you know about Faerie's infrastructure?"

"What kind of infrastructure? Because if you're talking about the spells that maintain the realm—"

"No, nothing like that. I mean, other than the King and Queen, who runs things? Their Majesties can't have time to make every decision, right?"

"Oh. There's a hierarchy, of course. It used to be more feudal. You know, the ell managed their minions—"

"The who?"

"The ell. In Faerie, gender is optional, so the person with power may or may not identify as a laird or lady. Ell."

"Got it. Thanks."

"Anyway, the ell was the authority over their little piece of the pie, regardless of the nature of the folk who made up the pie. But now it's more…species-based, I guess?"

"You mean like collective bargaining units? The brownies decide on their working conditions, the duergars theirs, the dryads theirs?"

"Exactly."

"Who coordinates it all? The King and Queen?"

"Nope. There are only certain things that need to get escalated to them if the parties can't come to an agreement. The

King's seneschal's office is sort of the clearing house for everything else."

The seneschal. Right. They'd been in charge of organizing Lachlan's sundering, the ceremony that severed his handfasting knot to his former husband. "How are disputes settled?"

She chuckled. "You mean other than with swords, fireballs, and hellhounds?"

"Hey!" Jordan protested. "Be careful how you use the H word."

"Sorry, Jordan," Eleri said. "Sorry, Doop."

"It's okay, Eleri," Jordan replied. "Doop's not here. We just all need to be sensitive about words, you know? Because they can hurt."

"Right. Sorry." She cleared her throat. "So why the questions about such a truly boring subject?"

"Well," I said, "it appears that I'm being sued."

"You're *what*?" she squawked. "By who?"

"I'm not sure."

"Oh, please." I could practically hear her eyeroll. "You're an investigator. You can do better than that. Is it a human lawsuit?"

"Since it was served by a redcap"—I patted Jordan's shoulder when he winced—"I'm thinking not."

She whistled. "A redcap. Damn. That's intense."

"Tell me about it," I muttered, "especially since I was naked at the time." When she practically shouted with laughter, I scowled at the phone. "Some BFF you are. I'd think you'd have more sympathy for my situation."

"Sorry, Hugh," she wheezed. "Really, I am. But you've got to admit it paints a very *evocative* picture." She took an audible breath. "Okay. I'm calm. Now open the damn summons and find out who's suing you. Maybe you're not the target at all. Maybe you're just being called as a witness."

The nerves dancing in my middle settled—fractionally. "That...that could be." Maybe I was freaking out over nothing. Process servers didn't only deliver lawsuit papers, right? Maybe this was related to a Quest case. We'd been hit with that rash of annoying thefts lately, and not all of our clients had been happy with the results—like that raven shifter who'd found out his brother-in-law was the one pilfering his vintage Beanie Babies. This might have nothing to do with me personally at all.

"Then open the damn thing already."

My fingers didn't shake—much—as I tore open the envelope. The papers inside were parchment, for Pete's sake. Jordan popped up from the chair and looked over my shoulder as I unfolded them. They crinkled in a *heavier* way than paper did, and an official-looking seal, complete with dangling red ribbons, adorned the bottom over a completely illegible—but very ornate—signature.

"'The party of the first part, Hugh Mann, aka Matthew Hadden Steinitz,'" Jordan murmured, then lifted his chin, eyes wide. "Wow, Hugh, they *three-named* you, with your *human* name."

My mouth went dry. "It's definitely a lawsuit." I scanned the document, squinting at the calligraphy with its uneven ink—clearly not written with a ballpoint or printed on a laser printer—looking for whoever was suing me. I frowned. "Who the heck is Yannick Tan?"

Jordan shrugged. "I don't recognize the name. Were they from one of your cases, Eleri?"

The three of us had been handling our raft of nuisance cases individually—well, individually for Eleri and me. Jordan always had Doop with him, and was absolutely thrilled to be a junior investigator, although we hadn't handed him anything that seemed too complicated or dangerous. However, he and Doop had a better close rate on cases involving missing items than Eleri or me.

"I don't recognize it either. Have you asked Zeke? He'll know all the clients, even the ones that Mal and Niall handle personally."

"We're kind of in the middle of the ocean right now." I glanced at the hatch. "With a literal boatload of selkies. But we'll try to get back soon. Meet us at the office? Maybe you can brief Zeke before we get there."

"I'll try. But I may not be able to slip away for a while. There's a vote coming up and I don't want to get stuck with another Illiam Coutts as clan leader."

"Okay. No worries. We'll—"

Jordan squeaked next to me and cut off the call. "Sorry," he whispered, "but they're coming back."

For a moment, I was afraid he meant the redcap, but then the selkie contingent boiled out of the hatch onto the deck. I stared at them. When I'd seen them from the transom, they'd all been dressed in more or less human-normal clothing appropriate for the weather. But now?

Every last one of them was in their seal skin with the hood lying back between their shoulders.

"Were they downstairs *stripping*?" Jordan murmured, clearly scandalized. "There's no *room*."

"Let's hope they were just wearing their pelts under their clothing." Because the notion that I'd been standing, bare-assed, above a hold full of naked selkies while a redcap slapped me with a lawsuit was not an image I wanted haunting my dreams. I mean, I get that shifters aren't that bothered by nudity, but I wasn't a shifter, and I preferred to choose who I shared skin with a little more intentionally.

I craned my neck, searching the crowd for Lachlan. Ordinarily he wasn't hard to spot, since he towered over most other people, as enormous as he was. However, it seemed that his physique was more or less common for selkies—all of them were built along mythic proportions, even not-Gandalf, who stepped forward, beaming like all the others. I don't think I'd ever been in a crowd this...joyful since the last time I'd gone to a Hunter's Moon concert.

Not-Gandalf was still gripping his staff, although now that I could see its base, I wasn't sure it was a walking stick at all. Yeah, its knotty handle was burnished with time and use, but intricately braided jute twine secured a thick bundle of twigs the length of my forearm to its bottom. It looked like a Halloween prop for a really tall witch—the human cosplay kind, not actual supe witches, who generally subscribed to a very different aesthetic.

He inclined his head to me. Not quite a bow, but definitely a gesture of respect. I shifted a little, my bare feet cold on the deck, feeling *way* underdressed. I mean, I was in worn jeans and these guys were all wearing freaking *fur*. Granted, they weren't garments, precisely, but they still looked shiny and soft and luxurious in a way my five-year-old North Face fleece did not.

"Master Steinitz," he said reverently.

I jerked at his use of my real name as the rest of the selkies echoed his words. This was the second time today that someone in the supe community had used it, when ordinarily Lachlan was the only one who ever called me anything other than *Hugh*.

"Uh…hello?"

"I am Calum MacGregor, Steward to the Throne and Keeper of Lore."

I could hear the capitalization of his titles in his ringing tones. "Pleased to meet you?" I still couldn't spot Lachlan.

"Hugh," Jordan murmured, "do you know what's going on?"

"No. And I'm not hanging around to find out." I turned my best professional smile on Calum. "Since you're here to meet with Lachlan, I'll leave you to it. Jordan and I can—"

"Nonsense," he said jovially. "We didn't come for His Majesty. We came for you."

"For me?"

"Of course." His smile grew even wider, if that was possible. It was…ominous somehow. I almost preferred the redcap's mouthful of pointed choppers. "We all wanted to be here to share the occasion."

I took a half step backward. "Occasion? What occasion?"

"Matthew!"

Lachlan shouldered his way through the crowd. He wasn't scowling, which was my first clue that something was wrong. In fact, I'd never seen him look this apologetic. And somehow, that and the helpless lift of his still-furred shoulder banished my wary embarrassment.

"What occasion are they talking about, Lachlan?" I said through clenched teeth. "Is there something you want to share with the class?"

CHAPTER FOUR

I took Lachlan's arm and angled him so we were facing away from the selkies. "Who are these people—and don't say *'They're selkies,'* because I know that already."

"Clan chiefs and other selkie officials."

"Like the Lord High Executioner over there?" I glanced sidelong at Calum, who'd moved nearer, probably the better to eavesdrop.

"Who?"

"Never mind." I huffed out a breath, my back crawling, because I could *feel* them sneaking closer. "You know what? Let's go below to have this conversation." I turned, but kept my gaze focused on Lachlan. "Because I don't want— *Agh!*"

I flailed, trying to keep my balance, because Calum's staff was *right there,* at my shin level, nearly swiping my feet out from under me.

"Matthew!" Lachlan grabbed my arm and somehow managed to help me stumble over the staff without both of us faceplanting on the deck.

A cheer, loud and joyous, rose from the selkies, and let me tell you, they've got *lungs* on them, probably from spending so much time holding their breath under water. They surged forward, and despite Lachlan's size and his shouted protests, hauled him out of the pilothouse and raised him onto their shoulders.

Then they turned toward me.

Nope nope nope. Whatever this was, I could tell I wasn't going to like it, so I bolted.

I don't know how I made it through the crowd—I suspected Jordan acted as a juggernaut, as weird as that sounds—to plunge through the hatch and stagger through the salon littered with discarded clothing into the relative safety of the berth. I dogged the door shut and tried to catch my breath.

"Hugh?" Jordan whispered from the other side of the door. "Sorry. I know you'd rather be alone. But I didn't want to stay up there with all of them, especially since they're all yelling at Lachlan again, so I'll just wait here, if that's okay."

"Sure, Jordan. No problem."

"Do you want some tea or something? I mean, I'm not Zeke, so it probably wouldn't be as good, but—"

"Nice of you, but no. Thanks, but no." I doubted I could have kept it down, anyway.

The heat in the berth that would have been welcome half an hour ago now had me shedding my jacket and pulling at the neck of my henley. I sank down on the edge of the mattress. "This day is *so* not delivering on my expectations."

All I'd wanted was to finally have sex with Lachlan in a nice comfy bed, with our privacy guaranteed by the whole freaking ocean.

I glared at the ceiling. I certainly hadn't banked on freezing my nuts off, flashing a bunch of strangers—not to mention a co-worker and my FTA driver—getting served with a lawsuit, and then nearly taking a header onto the deck. I mean, seriously? I'd done everything *except* sleep with Lachlan.

"Matthew?" Lachlan's voice was soft. "May I come in?"

I narrowed my eyes at the door. "You don't have the selkie posse with you, do you?"

"Nay. They won't leave, but I've ordered them to stay up on deck."

"Fine." I stood and unlatched the door, glaring at him when he loomed just outside, still in his seal skin, a decidedly sheepish expression on his face. "Okay, Lucy, you've got some 'splainin' to do."

His brow furrowed. "Lucy?"

I sighed. If supes truly wanted to blend in with the human world, they needed to brush up on their popular culture. "Never mind. Just come in."

He did, and when he turned to close the door, I spotted Jordan huddled on the padded banquette in the salon, gazing at us, eyes huge.

Nope. Nothing's happening in this bed today.

I planted myself on the bed again, and Lachlan sat next to me. "I'm sorry about that."

I squinted at him. "About what, exactly? Because there are quite a few things that could qualify as needing an apology."

He winced and ran both hands through his hair, which, I noted sourly, was still dry and fell in those perfect sun-streaked brown waves.

"Those bloody selkies," he grumbled. I noted that he'd had a similar reaction when they'd first arrived: annoyed, but not especially surprised.

"Were you expecting them?" I demanded.

He faced me, hurt banishing his scowl. "Not here. And not now."

"But you *did* expect them?"

"Aye." His shoulders slumped. "But I'd counted on more time."

"More time for what?"

"More time before I have to..." He sighed and propped his elbows on his thighs, his big hands dangling between his knees. "Before I have to leave."

My belly jolted, and not because the boat continued to rock. "Leave? You mean like on a visit?"

He laced his fingers together, not looking at me. "Nay. To return to Orkney. To take up the bloody throne."

"But…but you don't want to be their king."

He turned his head, his eyebrow quirked. "I don't. But I accepted their tribute, a tribute due only to a king."

"That damned ruby." I punched his arm. "I *told* you that wasn't necessary." When a Quest case had led us to Sheol, and I'd sort of vanished for a while, Lachlan had given a ruby the size of my fist to Paimon for my return. "I had everything under control. I returned myself *myself*." Myself along with Herne, his pack of Cwn Annwn, and the two jackasses—Athaniel and Melchom, angel and demon—who'd imagined they could cheat Lucifer.

"Aye. You did. But I didn't know that. And Matthew…" He turned and took both my hands. "…I'd have given more than that for your safety."

As much as that made my heart flutter, it also made my ears burn with anger. "You mortgaged your *life*, Lachlan. Committed to something you don't want, something you *never* wanted. How is that worth it?"

He shrugged. "You are worth everything, *mo cridhe*."

Okay, I gotta confess. When he said things like that, looked at me with such sincerity in his deep, dark eyes, I got a little swoony. You would too. I defy anyone to resist Lachlan Brodie when he's in full-on schmoopy mode. But…

"The thing is, Lachlan, that I don't consider your misery a fair price." I swallowed. "Especially if it takes you away."

He traced my cheek with one finger. "I knew what I was doing."

I batted his hand away. "Yeah, but *I* didn't know you were doing it. For decisions like that, don't you think we should, you know, *discuss* them first? Decide what's an acceptable compromise before you give away the farm?"

His eyebrows bunched. "I don't have a farm."

"Brother," I muttered.

"I knew what I was about, *mo cridhe*. I've made my bed." He winced. "And yours too, I fear."

My insides rocked like the freaking boat. "What's that supposed to mean?"

"Have I ever told you about how selkies wed?"

"Considering you're about as talkative as the average clam, that would be a big fat no. Is it a handfasting, like yours and Wyn's was?" Lachlan had only severed the knot with his fae ex-husband a couple of weeks ago, which was the reason we were finally free to have sex—assuming we were ever alone long enough to do the deed.

"Nay. As Wyn is fae, he wished to be married in the fae manner. We selkies...jump the besom."

"Besom?"

"What you might call a broom."

My jaw dropped. "You mean when we stumbled over that broomstick up there—"

"Aye." He took my hand, his expression strongly resembling Frang's just before he lunged for the railing. "We're married."

I leaped off the bed and backed up until I hit the wall. "No. No no no."

"Matthew—"

"Don't *Matthew* me!" I gripped my hair with both hands and tugged. Hard. "I don't *believe* this."

He had the nerve to look hurt. "I thought you wanted us to be together."

"I wanted us to *date*, Lachlan. To get to know each other better. To...to..." I flapped my hands at the bed. "To have sex. We've only known each other for two months, for Pete's sake."

"I knew in two minutes," he murmured.

I pointed squarely at his nose. "Don't. Don't try to pretend that you were that certain. Because, if you recall, you got married once before. You were probably just as certain about Wyn, too."

"I wasn't. But he wanted it, and I wanted to help."

I stared at him, my throat working until I finally managed to swallow. "Is that why you did this? Because you wanted to *help* the poor human with the obsession for all things supe? Did you *pity* me?"

His eyes widened in shock. "What? No! I don't pity you." He surged to his feet, but I threw up a hand before he could approach me. "I love you, Matthew. I thought you knew."

I forced myself to take a breath because my lungs were leaden in my chest. "How, precisely, would I have known? You've never actually *said* it." Neither had I, but I was on a roll and it was the *principle* of the thing.

He looked honestly surprised. "I haven't?"

"No. Trust me. I'd have remembered." I shook my head, but it didn't help to clear my mind. "Jeez, Lachlan, you only stopped calling me *lad* two weeks ago."

"I'm sorry, Matthew. I—" He spread his palms. I wasn't sure if it was a gesture of surrender or to show me he didn't have anything else up his sleeve. "I've been told I'm not the best at communicating."

"You *think*?"

"But I should have told you that. Every day. Often. So you would have no doubt. Dare I—" He gazed at me, eyes soft with what looked like hope. "Dare I hope you feel the same for me?"

I gritted my teeth, because I was still mad, but I couldn't lie to him. "Yes," I barked. "You know I do."

His smile lit the whole cabin. "Then we have no problem."

"We have nothing *but* problems. Because, in case you forgot to communicate *that* as well, you never asked me to marry you."

He had the grace to look ashamed. "I know. I intended to once we'd had our swim. I didn't expect the selkies to arrive so soon."

"Did you expect them to bring their freaking *broom*?"

"Nay. But I told you. I've got to take the throne." He bit his lip, his gaze sliding away to study the oh-so-fascinating space heater. "And as my consort, you'll have duties, too."

"Oh, hell no." I edged along the wall, keeping well away from him. "You supes *really* have to work on the concept of consent."

He nodded glumly. "Aye. I ken that. If you wish, we can jump back over the besom and you'll be shed of me."

I frowned. "You mean that's all it takes to get selkie-divorced?"

"Aye. If Calum hasn't left with the besom, we could do it now, and you'd have no ties to me. You'd be free after I'm gone."

I froze with one hand on the door latch. "You'd be back, though, right?"

He shook his head. "Nay. I'm pledged to the clans now. I'll have to sell the *Cridhe na Mara* and move back to Scotland."

"But why?" A pit had opened in my belly at the notion of never seeing Lachlan again. Yeah, I was freaked and irritated by the selkie shotgun wedding, but that didn't mean I wanted to break up completely. "You could use the FTA to travel to your palace—"

He snorted. "Hardly a palace. More a stone longhouse. With a thatched roof."

"Sounds cozy." Not. "You could show up there for regular royal office hours, but spend your nights here." *With me.* "I mean, other couples have jobs that keep them apart during the day. Look at Mal, Niall, and Zeke."

Lachlan shook his head. "That's not how the selkie rulership works. Think of the King and Queen of Faerie. They must always be available to their subjects, to help and guide them. That's what I must do."

"But you hate the idea of them even needing a king."

"Aye. I do. Especially a king the likes of me. But I pledged to do it when I accepted the tribute."

"And you always keep your promises," I grumbled.

"We can go above now and jump back." He smiled crookedly. "I'd never ask you to do something you didn't want to do, *mo cridhe.*"

"I seem to remember you asking me to leap into the Pacific Ocean, naked, in November, so that won't exactly fly."

His eyes widened. "As to that—"

"Never mind." I rested my hands on his chest, the steady rhythm of his heart calming my nerves. "Look. I'm not happy about the besom ambush, but that wasn't entirely your fault. I'm not ready to call it quits between us because of some arcane selkie tradition."

Another glorious smile, dammit. "You're not?"

"No. But I'm also not ready to eighty-six my life for a gig I know nothing about." I glanced at the closed door. "Do you have to go with them now?"

He nodded. "There are some disputes to mediate. Some arrangements to make for our"—he swallowed—"for my accommodations."

"Well, stall them as long as you can with stupid little details and demands."

He frowned. "I don't have any demands."

"Well, *get* some. You're the king. Throw your authority around. But whatever you do"—I jabbed my finger into his chest—"*don't* make any more promises."

"If it means you'll stay with me—"

"I'll *think* about it, okay? We'll *talk.*" I heaved a sigh. "But for now, I need to get back to Quest."

He frowned. "But you had the whole day free."

"That was before a redcap showed up and slapped me with a lawsuit from somebody I've never heard of."

"A redcap?" There was that familiar scowl. "Threatened you? On *my boat*?"

"Yep. Seems he hitched a ride with the selkies when they popped out of Faerie and onto the deck." I started to grin. "You know, that might be something you could leverage. They let a redcap come into their king's presence. Seems that would be a big no-no."

If my grin was evil, Lachlan's was positively feral. "Aye. And a prime reason that I'd not trust my consort in their presence." He edged closer, a question in his eyes. "Matthew? May I?"

I'm not a total fool, okay? Of course I kissed him. But only once. Okay, five times, but kept it as innocent as I could, given that we were inches away from a bed. "Let me know how it goes, all right?" When he nodded, I undogged the door and stepped into the salon.

Jordan immediately jumped to his feet, glancing worriedly between me and Lachlan. "Um...everything okay?"

I grimaced. The berth's "door" wasn't more than a stiffened canvas curtain. Jordan had probably heard every word I'd hurled at Lachlan. "Sure." I listened for noises on deck. "The selkies still up there?"

"Some of them." He ducked and peered through the hatch. "I think they're taking turns diving into the water, but some of them are always up there in the pilothouse." He straightened and whispered, "I've been checking."

I sighed. I wasn't ready to face any of them, not now, and maybe not ever, depending on whether Lachlan and I could untangle his unwanted commitments. On the other hand, I may not have the choice if this lawsuit landed me in supe jail, aka Govannon's forge, or even worse, gave the council the excuse to wipe my memory and send me back to my mundane human existence.

"If you use Hector's illegal FTA app, do you think you could call a driver here? Below deck?"

He scrunched up his face. "If I request a subcompact, sure." He brightened. "I'll make sure they're water-based too, so they won't...you know...all over Lachlan's boat."

Lachlan chuckled. "I'd appreciate that, laddie."

"All right then." I took a deep breath. "Let's go."

CHAPTER
FIVE

Our driver, a diminutive fae—who Jordan said in one of his unsubtle stage whispers was a mari-morgan, but I shouldn't worry because she didn't drown people anymore—safely delivered us to the portal that led to the fourth floor corridor in Quest's offices. When we stepped through, though, I smacked headfirst into a—one by twelve?

"Ow!" I rubbed my nose. "What the..."

"Shit!" A man rivaling Ted and Lachlan in height and breadth, brown-haired and red-bearded, dressed construction chic complete with tool belt, hurried over to me. Behind me, Jordan uttered a strangled whimper, because the man was Rusty Johnson, contractor, inactive beaver shifter, and the subject of Jordan's latest crush. "Are you okay, Hugh?" He frowned at the guy carrying the boards. "Ronnie, I warned you to walk in the middle of the hallway."

Ronnie swung around and would have beaned his boss if Rusty hadn't blocked the board with his palm. "Sorry, Rusty. I forgot." Ronnie shot me a cheeky grin. "All right there, Hugh?"

"Sure, Ronnie." I stopped rubbing my nose and forced a smile. "No problem."

As Ronnie continued down the hall—once more drifting toward the wall instead of staying in the center—Rusty shook his head. "If his brother wasn't such a key member of my crew,

I'm not sure I'd let Ronnie within ten miles of any of my job sites."

I could understand Rusty's reservations. Ronnie Purl put the *shifty* in *shifter*. His ferret nature gave him severe impulse control issues around anything soft, which had gotten him into trouble in the past. But I could also understand why Rusty kept giving him second, third, and fifty-seventh chances. Ronnie was light-fingered and twitchy, but he was good-hearted about it and sincerely loved his brother, Devin.

When Ronnie took a wide turn onto the stairs to the top floor, the boards smacked into the wall, leaving a noticeable dent. Rusty winced. "Guess I'd better put wall repair on my punch list." He smiled at Jordan. "Hey, Jordan. How's it going?"

"Fine." Jordan's voice was about two octaves higher than normal.

"Pup not with you today?"

"No." Jordan swallowed. "He's at the Dog House."

Rusty chuckled. "Probably best. There'll be a lot of strangers and unfamiliar noises around here for a while. Wouldn't want him to be uncomfortable."

Devin Purl hurried by carrying a spool of some kind of cable, followed by a couple of guys hefting sheets of drywall. "You're renovating Zeke's old apartment? Already?" I asked. Mal and Niall had decided to convert the space into a more cushy staff lounge, since the one we'd arranged in an old slate-walled workroom had enough residual magic imbued in its walls that I always felt like somebody was looking over my shoulder.

Rusty nodded. "I didn't think we'd be able to start until spring, but one of my human clients had their financing fall through, so we had an unexpected opening. This job's not too extensive, so we shouldn't be in your hair for too long." He nodded at me, slapped Jordan on the shoulder, and strode off to disappear up the stairs.

Jordan sighed. "He's just so...so..."

I raised my eyebrows. "Married?" To a vampire, no less. Then I winced. Apparently, I was sort of married now too.

Jordan frowned at me. "I'd never *do* anything, any more than he would. But you can admire somebody without there being anything sketchy about it. You know. Just because they're *admirable*." He sighed. "Besides, *looking* and *admiring* are a lot less complicated than *doing*."

"Tell me about it," I muttered as I headed for the stairs.

"Oh, Hugh!" Jordan scuttled to catch up with me and held out an altogether too familiar envelope. "You left this in the pilothouse. I figured you wouldn't want it to blow overboard or for those selkies to snoop in it."

I reluctantly took the papers, since ignoring them wouldn't make them go away. "Thanks. Are selkies especially snoopy?"

He shrugged as we descended the stairs, the sounds of hammering and the whine of power tools filtering down from above. "Not any more than anybody else." Then he grinned. "But with supes, that's not saying much."

"Good point." I suspected that my unexpected broom nuptials would be common knowledge before we hit the lobby.

When we reached Zeke's desk, though, he didn't immediately congratulate me. Instead, his dark eyes were wide behind the bespelled glasses that compensated for his Sheol-adapted eyesight. "Hugh." His voice was barely audible. "There's somebody waiting for you in the Little Conference Room."

Just what I needed. More unexpected visitors. "Anybody I know?"

Zeke slid a business card across the desk. It was black, which, you know, should have given me a clue. I picked it up and flipped it over. The other side was mostly black, too, except for the white outline of a figure in a hooded cloak gripping a scythe in both hands.

Jordan peered over my shoulder. "*Death* is waiting for Hugh upstairs?"

Zeke waggled one hand. "More...death adjacent?"

I laid the card back on the desk because it was giving me the creeps. "If they're an undertaker, they need to seriously work on their branding."

Eleri strolled in, and from the purple Wonderful Mug to-go cup in her hand, I guessed Jordan wasn't the only one who'd encountered a secret—or maybe not-so-secret—crush this morning.

"What did I miss?"

"What makes you think you missed anything?"

"For one thing, there's practically a visible thundercloud over your head and Jordan doesn't have his attendant hellhound."

For once Jordan didn't chastise Eleri for using the H word. "Death's come for Hugh!"

"You're dying?" Eleri aimed the cup in the general direction of Zeke's desk and let go—only Zeke's demon super-speed reflexes saved it from upending onto his desk blotter. Then she flung herself at me, hugging me tight around the waist. "Oh, Hugh. Why didn't you say something?"

"I'm not dying." I patted her back absently, my gaze snagged on that ominous black business card again. "Or not any more than I ever am. You know, short-lived human among long-lived supes and all that?"

She let go of me, darting glances between me, Jordan, and Zeke. "Explain."

Zeke pointed to the business card with one hand and held Eleri's rescued latte out with the other. "He's not Death, precisely. He's an Ankou."

Eleri accepted the cup. "A what now?"

"An Ankou. A Breton psychopomp."

Jordan's eyes grew as round as one of his beloved Frisbees. "You mean like a serial killer?" he breathed.

"Not a psycho*path*," Zeke said patiently. "A psycho*pomp*. A being whose task it is to escort the deceased."

I frowned. "Escort them where?"

"Onward." Zeke spread both hands, palms up. "Wherever or whatever that might be. We used to see them in Sheol sometimes, although usually the souls who'd contracted with demons had forfeited their right to move on. Occasionally, though, the contract had a time limit, and the soul was allowed to leave, but only in the company of a psychopomp."

I itched for my notebook so I could jot down these facts. "Are Ankous the only ones with the job?"

"Oh, no. Nearly every culture has someone with a similar function. Generally, the dead are assigned to the psychopomp relative to their own culture and belief system."

"And Ankous are Breton, you said? I thought they'd all disappeared." In fact, investigating the disappearance of Cornish, Manx, and Breton fae was the reason Quest had been founded in the first place.

"Some came out of hiding," Jordan said. "Our FTA driver just now was a Breton."

"That's true." Eleri took a sip of her latte. "They heard about the regime change somehow and came knocking on Faerie's door to see if it was all true. There's still not many of them around, though."

"If there are so few Breton fae, this Ankou must not have many customers."

"Psychopomps guide human souls as well as supes. More, in fact, since there are so many more humans and they—" Jordan cut a glance at me and hung his head.

"They die in such droves?" I patted his shoulder. "It's okay, Jordan. I've said it myself more than once."

Zeke folded his hands atop his blotter. "Psychopomps generally assist the dead from their own culture, but they're not prevented from escorting anyone who's eligible to move on."

Could this Ankou have a lead, a link to the Disappeared? Maybe a visit from Death would be a good thing. I mean, this day couldn't possibly get worse. "Does this guy have a case for us?"

"I'm…not sure. He asked for you by name, though."

Interesting. I glanced at the envelope in my hand and phantom caterpillars crept up my spine. "Which name?"

Zeke's brows quirked in surprise. "Actually, both. I didn't notice that, but it's unusual."

I clenched my eyes shut. "This guy's name doesn't happen to be Yannick Tan, does it?"

Zeke's expression cleared and he smiled. "Yes! How did you know?"

I waggled the envelope. "Because apparently he's suing me."

"What?" The outrage in Zeke's tone was gratifying, I've gotta say. "Are those the papers?" At my nod, he thrust out a hand. "Let me review them. If they have anything to do with a Quest case, he has no grounds. Your actions are covered by our E&O insurance policy, which was drawn up by the C-Suite demons, and they *never* leave loopholes."

I passed him the envelope. "That would be great, Zeke. Thanks." I tugged on the hem of my henley. My skin was itchy from residual salt water, but there wasn't much I could do about it now. As late as yesterday, I'd have run up to Zeke's old apartment and used the shower. But the shower might already be history. I'd watched enough HGTV to know how enthusiastically construction workers approached demo day. I'd just have to face Death as I was.

"Do you want me to come with you, Hugh?" Jordan didn't sound thrilled with the notion, and his shoulders were tense, as though he were bracing for a blow. "Well, me and Eleri. Or maybe just Eleri, since she's your BFF and everything."

"Actually," Zeke said, "we have another theft case that could benefit from both Jordan and Eleri since the theft occurred in Forest Park. Trees and tracking. Your specialties." With a smile, he passed Eleri a manila folder. "The clients would appreciate a quick return of the stolen property. I told them they had nothing to worry about with you two on the case."

Eleri tossed her empty cup away. "Okay, kiddo." She nudged Jordan with her elbow. "Guess it's you and me."

"Really?" Relief flickered over Jordan's face, replaced by pride. "We'll get right on it, Zeke. You can count on us." He gave me an apologetic smile. "Sorry, Hugh. You understand, though, right?"

"Sure. Good luck, guys."

Jordan bounded out of the room and up the stairs toward the portal. "Come on, Eleri! We don't want to lose the trail."

Eleri lifted an eyebrow at Zeke. "Is this really a rush case?"

Zeke's blush blotched the fair skin of his neck and throat. "No. But I could tell he was uncomfortable with meeting Yannick."

"Zeke, my dear," Eleri said with a shake of her head, "with a heart that big, you must have been a truly terrible demon." She sauntered out of the room.

Zeke ducked his head, his blush still raging. He fussed with the envelope, removing the papers and spreading them across his blotter. "I'll scan these and send them on to our advocate for a closer review, then join you upstairs with more refreshments. Unless you'd rather I accompany you now?"

"No." I tapped the corner of one parchment page. "I'd much prefer to know what my options are with the suit. Since I'm not dead, it's not like Yannick can carry me off to someplace beyond. I'm sure I'll be fine." Annoyed, aggravated, and angry, but fine. My biggest challenge would be trying to reason with the guy before I started yelling at him.

I left Zeke poring over the documents and headed up to my office on the third floor. I hung my jacket on the wall hook and grabbed my camera bag, but then I caught sight of myself in the mirror on the back of the door. My hair was standing up on one side, one of the buttons was hanging off my henley by a thread, and I'd missed my last belt loop. Jeez, way to look professional.

On the one hand, I didn't much care how I came across to Yannick Tan, the suer. On the other, did I really want to greet Death looking like I was one step away from derelict?

I ducked into the restroom and made myself as presentable as possible by changing into one of the spare shirts I kept in the office, wetting my hair and wrestling it into submission with a fine-toothed comb, and rebuckling my belt properly. But the effort was for my own self-respect, not for Mr. Death-and-Legal-Destruction.

I headed for the Little Conference Room, forcing myself into a confident, unhurried stride. I paused in the doorway to scope out the scene. Zeke had arranged the standard refreshments on the credenza—bottled water, scones, and tea in the pot with the spout shaped like a Welsh dragon's snout—and laid a fresh legal pad and several pens on the table in my usual spot.

Yannick Tan wasn't awaiting me there, although there was an empty teacup and a plate littered with crumbs in front of one chair. Instead, he was standing at the window, his back to the door. Contrary to what his business card suggested, he wasn't dressed in a hooded cloak, nor were there any ominous farm implements in evidence. The only black he was wearing was an Oakley ball cap—backwards. Otherwise, his outfit consisted of faded jeans, high-top basketball sneakers with their laces untied, and an oversized green camo hoodie. In other words, not so much Death as Ennui.

"Yannick Tan? I believe you asked to see me?"

He turned unhurriedly and stared at me, his lip lifting in a sneer. "Hugh Mann," he said, voice dripping with disdain. "Ready to settle, troublemaker?"

Troublemaker? I took my time collecting a bottle of water. After I sat down, I took a long swallow and picked up a pen. "Suppose you tell me exactly what your problem is and we'll discuss it rationally."

"*My* problem?" He strode to the table and slapped it with both palms. "I didn't *have* a problem until you poked your nose where it didn't belong." He pushed off the table again and paced the length of the room. "Not many Bretons adhere to the old ways anymore. I was called to one or two a month. Three at most."

I frowned at him. "And that's a problem?"

"No, that's not the problem. I had plenty of time to kick back with a brewski. Play *Call of Duty*. Binge-watch K-dramas."

Him playing *Call of Duty* was a bit ironic, considering he was refusing his own duty call. "Let me get this straight. You're Slacker Death?"

He jabbed a forefinger at me. "Hey! I *earned* this slowdown. I've had this gig since the beginning, and I was due the rest, know what I'm saying? Then suddenly I'm overrun by souls, all wanting my attention, and most of 'em aren't even Breton!"

"In other words, you've been asked to do your job?"

"Not *my* job. *Everyone's* job. I'm the only Ankou left. The rest of them cut out years ago when the demand decreased."

"I'm still not entirely sure how this has anything to do with me."

He glared at me, eyes sparking red. "*You* showed up in Sheol and *saw* them. They *saw* you seeing them. And then you did *something* that let them loose. Now all of them are knocking on my door, swarming my crib, *standing in front of my wide-screen TV.*"

"Devastating," I said, deadpan.

"Dude, you have no idea." He flopped into a chair. "The paperwork alone is killer."

"Intense?"

"Majorly. Some of these jokers made their deals in the Middle Ages. They don't even know *where* to move on now. And none of them can make a decision to save their lives." He drummed his fingers on the table, squinting one eye. "Although it's probably a little late for that, anyway."

"I'm still not sure why you're after me about it. *I* didn't entrap the souls there. That was their own doing, along with general demon chicanery. I'd heard most of the souls were awaiting case reviews anyway, and the tribunal had a backlog."

"Yeah, but apparently your stunt with the dimensional pocket showed them that the demons were burying the release requests. If the demons weren't playing by the rules, the dead decided they didn't need to, either. They lodged a petition with the supe council and"—he bunched his fists and then extended his fingers in jazz hands—"boom."

"It still has nothing to do with me. Shouldn't you be taking this up with the Sheol C-suite or the supe council?"

"You think I'm stupid? Negotiating with demons is what got these losers in trouble in the first place." He thrust out his lower lip like a pouting toddler. "And the supe council would probably just tell me to suck it up."

"So why don't you?"

"Why don't I what?"

"Suck it up and do your job. These souls have been waiting a long time. Don't you think they're due resolution? A final rest?"

He glared at me. "What about *my* final rest, huh? When do *I* catch a break?"

I forbore from stating that he'd had a pretty cushy existence for quite a while. "I still don't see why you're targeting me in this suit. I was acting on behalf of Quest Investigations."

"Right," he scoffed. "Like I can sue the King's brother, or the Queen's old enforcer."

"In other words"—I tapped my pencil on the legal pad, fast, faster, fastest—"you picked me because I'm human, and therefore of least importance?"

"Well. Yeah." He rolled his eyes. "*Ob*viously."

My ears started to burn. "And *that* is why I'm not about to help you. You're a victimizer, Mr. Tan, when you should be a facilitator. Blaming somebody else for your inconvenience doesn't resolve the problem, not for you, and not for the souls desperate for your services."

"But I *can't*," he whined. "There are so many of them and they won't. Stop. *Picking* at me."

"Then *help* them," I roared. "That's what you're supposed to do, isn't it?"

"But not all at *once*. I can't even— When I try to talk to one of them, a dozen others start complaining that I should help them first. And then I try to help one of *them* and the first one hangs off my leg, cursing and wailing."

Zeke appeared in the doorway with a tea tray, this pot painted like Van Gogh's *Starry Night*. "Leaving the souls to their own devices is *not* an option."

My eyebrows shot up. Zeke's tone rivaled Bryce's druid power voice, the one that made everybody within earshot hop to it. "Why?"

His lips pressed together in a tight line, but the rattle of the tray as he plonked it on the table was the true giveaway— Zeke's tea service was never anything but fluid and silent. "Because if they're not managed, if they're not helped to move on, they'll go…elsewhere."

CHAPTER SIX

"Zeke? You okay?"

He hesitated for a moment, but then jerked a nod and clutched a chair back, his knuckles even whiter than usual. "We haven't had many cases involving untethered souls, but believe me when I tell you that they can wreak havoc if they've a mind to."

"What exactly do you mean by *havoc*?"

Zeke ran a shaking hand through his curls. "Think about it, Hugh. The souls relegated to Sheol are there because they struck a bargain with a demon, a bargain with an extremely steep price."

"Their soul."

He nodded. "Why be willing to pay that price unless what you expected to gain was something you coveted desperately, something you couldn't achieve with your own efforts, something to which you weren't entitled?"

"So…not exactly model citizens."

"Those who trade eternal torment for Upper World advantage—which is, by definition, transient—are rarely selfless." His brow wrinkled. "Although one could argue that having one's soul stripped is the definition of selfless, since it denotes removal of self."

"Philosophical questions aside, what are you afraid of?" Because Zeke *was* afraid. If I read him right, he was downright terrified.

His throat worked as though he were fighting nausea. "If those souls had another chance at what they craved, don't you think they'd grab it?"

I rolled my pen over my knuckles as I turned that thought over in my mind. "You mean, if someone wanted riches—"

"They might steal."

"If somebody wanted information?"

"They might spy."

"If someone wanted love?" I shuddered. "No, let's not go there."

"But, Hugh," he said, barely above a whisper, "what if they wanted revenge?"

Okay, now *that* was scary. "But souls aren't corporeal, right?" The ones I'd spotted through my special camera lens—long story—hadn't even been visible to anybody else until I'd snapped a photo.

"Under most circumstances, yes. But a lot depends on their relative strength of will and the…needs of the contracting demon."

"Needs," I muttered. "It's always about sticking it to the working stiff, isn't it?" That's probably why the souls in the Sheol Reception and Disposal office—longer story—had been able to manipulate the telephones and typewriters: Management needed clerical staff to do the grunt work. But Sheol was another realm, with different physical rules. "Could they manipulate objects here in the Upper World? Touch"—I swallowed—"people? Would they be like ghosts?"

"Define ghost." Zeke sighed. "If a ghost is what remains after a person dies, yet has not passed the final portal, then I suppose the Sheol-bound souls are synonymous. But ghosts who manifest spontaneously in the Upper World might be different."

"If they didn't contract with a demon, you mean? If they're just hanging around for some other reason?" I turned to Yannick, who was kicked back in his chair with his feet on the table, playing a game on his phone. "Yo, Mr. Death. Do you escort garden-variety ghosts too?"

"Not my problem." He didn't bother to look up. "Those are paranormal, not supernatural. They don't *want* to move on."

I blinked. There was *more* out there? Beyond, or rather adjacent to, the supe community? I put the question aside for now, because with everything else that had happened today, it was officially TMI. Besides, after my broom-jump wedding to a selkie, I was a member of the supe community by marriage anyway, and Yannick was failing us in a major way.

"Have you escorted *anybody* lately?"

He shot me the stink-eye before he returned to his game. "I told you. They won't let me."

"You mean you haven't tried," I growled. "If you—"

A yell and a clatter sounded from upstairs, followed by more shouting and a tortured scream.

I pushed away from the table and sprinted for the door. "I'll be back," I tossed at Yannick over my shoulder. "Don't move."

I galloped up the stairs, Zeke at my heels, to the fourth floor job site. I glanced around wildly for Rusty, but there was no sign of him, and he was as impossible to miss as Lachlan. Devin Purl and another worker I didn't recognize were feverishly shifting a jumbled mound of lumber.

"Devin? What happened?"

"Ronnie's under here." He and the other guy tossed two-by-fours aside like they were toothpicks. "Something happened with the circular saw. He lost control for some reason and — Ronnie? Can you hear me?"

Zeke and I rushed over to lend our hands to the recovery effort. "Jeez," I said as we heaved more wood aside, "how big was this pile?"

"Big," Devin said. "We have to replace all the studs and joists. Ronnie? Say something, man." There was a groan from under the pile. "Ronnie!"

We redoubled our efforts. "Where's Rusty?"

"He had to check on another job. Octavio here is the site foreman."

"Have either of you contacted Rusty or called the SMTs?"

"Shit," Octavio said. "No. Trying to dig Ronnie out first."

"I'll take care of it." Zeke moved aside, pulling out his cell phone as Ronnie moaned again.

"We're coming, Ronnie!" Devin cried. "Hold on!"

We managed to uncover Ronnie's head, chest, and one arm. I winced. Elbows were *not* supposed to bend in that direction— nor were they located in the middle of a forearm. Ronnie's eyes were closed, and he was breathing rapidly. There was a bump the size of a golf ball on his forehead, but I didn't see any blood. Not yet anyway.

Zeke hunkered down next to me and helped me shift boards off where Ronnie's other arm ought to be. "The SMTs are on their way. Octavio, Rusty wants you to secure the job site for the accident review inspectors, please. He'll meet you"—we uncovered Ronnie's right arm and hand, which was amazingly still clutching the circular saw—"at the hospital in a—"

"Look out!" I pushed Zeke aside as Ronnie convulsed, his spasm somehow switching the saw back on. I sucked in a breath at the burn of pain across my ribs as Zeke and I tumbled across the raw plywood subflooring.

"Hugh!" Zeke propped himself on both elbows, his eyes huge. "You're bleeding!"

I pushed myself back onto my knees—or tried to, because *up* was suddenly a relative direction.

I looked down at my side. My nice clean shirt now sported a very unfashionable gash, matching the one on my skin. "Oh." I pointed at one of three wavery Zekes. "Whatever you do," I said as my vision went dark, "don't mention this to Lachlan."

CHAPTER
SEVEN

My side burned. How— Did I run into another fire mage? I didn't remember—

"Hugh? All right there, mate?"

I opened my eyes to find Mal peering down at me, worry in his cobalt eyes.

"I, um…" I squinted in the bright lights. Judging from the low metal railings on either side of me and the blue-flowered curtain surrounding us, I was lying on a gurney in the St. Stupid's ER. The thin hospital johnny replacing my regular clothes was a big freaking clue, too. "Ow?"

Mal chuckled, but it was a little strained. "Gave us quite a scare for a mo, there. What were you thinking?"

I closed my eyes again. "About what?"

"You threw yourself into the breach. Putting your body between Zeke's and a circular saw blade."

"Oh." I took a shaky breath. "Right. I didn't want Zeke to get hurt."

Mal huffed, clearly exasperated, which I could understand. He needed his employees ambulatory. "Mate, he's a demon. He's practically indestructible. You, however, are not." He gripped my forearm. "I appreciate the effort, as does Zeke and, not incidentally, Hamish, who's hovering over him like a kangaroo nanny." Mal chuckled again. "Seems he takes exception to his boyfriend being up in that apartment space again, let alone in close proximity to implements of torture."

"It was a circular saw, not an implement of torture."

"In Sheol, *anything* can be an implement of torture in the right hands."

The curtain rings rattled as the drape was pushed aside, revealing Dr. Astell, the oracle ER doctor. "Oh. The human. Why isn't he in the ER for *his* kind?" He yanked the curtain closed again, with himself on the other side.

"Bloody wanker," Mal grumbled. He pulled out his cell phone. "I'm calling my brother-in-law."

"David? Why?" Mal's brother-in-law, my friend David, was an *achubydd*, a magical healer who could work wonders with supe injuries by interacting directly with their *calons*, the organ that was the seat of their supernatural nature. I pulled the blanket that covered me to the waist up to my chest, where I most definitely did *not* have a *calon*. "He can't affect humans."

"Not as much. But don't forget, he's a nurse, too. He can work a little first aid magic on you, even if Dr. Asshole can't be bothered."

"Is Ronnie okay?"

"The SMTs got him stabilized, but he was out cold last I checked." He glared at the curtain, which fluttered gently from the movement of the medimagical staff on the other side. "Dr. Asshole should be seeing to him next, if Rusty has anything to say about it." He smirked. "And he does. Rusty and Casimir are major hospital benefactors now, and Dr. Asshole always has his eye on the main chance."

"Money talks, huh?"

"Money and vampire status. Dr. Asshole is also a snob."

"Do tell." Clearly, the good doctor was not a fan of humans.

The curtain rattled again and David rushed in. "Hugh! Oh my gosh, are you okay?"

I pointed to my side. "Just a bit ventilated."

Comparing David's scowl to Lachlan's was kind of like comparing a kitten to a rabid lion, but I could tell David was seriously pissed off. "I'm going to have *words* with Dr. Astell. He should have—"

"No, it's okay. Ronnie's injuries were more serious than mine." I winced, remembering his arm.

"At least all his blood remained on the *inside*." He donned a pair of nitrile gloves with a snap. "Now, let's see what I can do." He paused, hands in the air, eyebrows quirked. "May I raise your gown? I'll keep the blanket covering your lower body."

"Sure." Apparently it was my day for flashing skin at my friends and co-workers, not to mention an entire pod of selkies. I hiked the gown up myself, catching a breath when it caught on whatever was going on along my ribs.

His fingers were gentle as he palpated my skin. "Hmmm. Not too bad. Shallow." He grinned at me. "No bone trauma." He stripped off the gloves and tossed them aside. "Although if you'd gone to a human hospital, you'd probably have at least twenty-five stitches." He scrubbed his hands at the sink. "Luckily, you're here with me, so no needles required." He waggled his fingers. "I'll need to touch your skin directly, no gloves in the way. Is that okay with you?"

"I can stand it if you can."

I expected him to put his hands over the wound, which, okay, ewww. But instead he took both my hands in his, his brows bunched in concentration. "It's different with humans," he murmured. "With supes, the energy I can access is driven by the *calon*. Internal. Intrinsic. Human energy is superficial, like an invisible skin. I can't go more than dermis deep, because there's nothing underneath for me to latch onto." His smile was a little strained. "That's why I can't really treat humans magically for severe internal injury or disease."

I frowned when his brows drew together. "Is this hurting you? If something happens to you—"

"No, no. It's just…weird. It should be harder for me to—"

"Where is he?"

David jerked a little, but quickly regained his focus. I sighed, because I recognized that bellow. *Lachlan.*

"My mate is here, and I demand to see him. Now."

Mal lifted an eyebrow. "Mate, is it?"

I sighed as warmth spread over my side where pain had been moments before. "Long story. But I asked Zeke not to tell him."

"Boyo," Mal said with a chuckle, "haven't you learned by now that where you're concerned, Lachlan Brodie can't resist sticking his big flipper into the business, whether it's any of his or not?"

The curtain was flung aside, and Lachlan loomed there with a nurse wearing an almost identical scowl hovering at his shoulder.

"Mr. Brodie, I told you. Unless Mr. Mann specifically requests —"

"It's okay," I said tiredly. "Let him in." I glared at Lachlan. "I doubt anyone could stop him."

The nurse glanced from David—whom she obviously knew, because she gave him a friendly nod—to Mal, to Lachlan. "Only two in the bay at once, if you please."

Mal stood. "I'll take myself off then." He neatly blocked Lachlan's approach to grip my shoulder. "Take all the time you need, Hugh. We'll totter on the best we can without you until you're feeling more the thing." He left, closing the curtain behind him in a rattle of metal.

"*Mo cridhe,*" Lachlan murmured. "Why didn't you call me?"

"Because I didn't want this exact thing to happen." I glared at him. "Fuss."

"Fuss?" His eyebrows obviously couldn't decide if they wanted to bunch over his eyes or disappear into his hairline, because they made the round trip a couple of times. "Is that what you call my concern?"

"No, that's what I call you barging into the ER and disrupting the place with your bellow."

His eyebrows settled in the downward—way downward—position. "When you don't tell me that you've nearly *died*—"

"Nothing so dire," David said. "In fact, you're good as new, although the site may be tender for a few days."

Lachlan glared at David, who deflected it with a sunny smile. "He should rest, though? In bed? No activity for a week or two?"

"Not necessary." David waved Lachlan's words away, clearly not in the least intimidated. But then, his husband was just as big, and usually carried a broadsword to boot. "Hugh, you know your own limits. You're free to do as much or as little as you feel able to do. But from the perspective of the injury itself, you're fully healed." He washed his hands again. "I'll take care of the discharge paperwork, so you can leave as soon as you like." He whisked out of the cubicle, the curtain billowing in his wake.

Lachlan rested one giant hand against my check. "*Mo cridhe,* you cannot frighten me so. Not before we've taken our swim."

I looked at him sourly. "Oh, I like that." I pushed myself up, fully expecting a twinge in my side, but...nothing. What can I say? David was good. "First you're worried that I'll expire from a little cut—"

"Little?" he growled. "That bloody ferret shifter took a saw to your ribcage!"

"He didn't mean to. He was barely conscious at the time. I'll be—" *Wait a minute.* Why waste an opportunity this, well, opportune? I pressed a hand to my side with a fake wince. "Although I'm pretty sure I won't feel up to that swim for a while." Maybe until July, when the air stood a chance at being warmer even if the water was still frigid.

"But, Matthew—"

I slapped my forehead. "Crap! Could you hand me my clothes, please? I've got Death waiting for me back at the Quest offices."

Lachlan's expression could have turned a fire demon to ice. "Don't jest about this, Matthew. If you're still in danger—"

"No, I mean I've got a client who's what Zeke calls death-adjacent. An Ankou." I grimaced. "Who's suing me."

"What?" Lachlan's bellow rattled the curtain rings and brought the stern nurse back.

"I don't mean to rush you, Mr. Mann," she said, brisk and no-nonsense, although her laser glare at Lachlan was less than friendly, "but Mr. Evans-Kendrick has completed your paperwork. If you're ready, one of our orderlies would be pleased to escort you to the exit."

In other words, get Lachlan out of her ER.

"I'll escort him," Lachlan rumbled, earning him another glare.

Before they could set each other ablaze, I slid off the gurney, keeping my back with the peek-a-boo gown away from the onlookers. "I'm fine. I'll go as soon as I'm dressed."

Her expression softened when she looked at me. "It's just that generally Mr. Evans-Kendrick's patients don't need much recovery time." She glanced over her shoulder as a couple of SMTs rushed by with another gurney. "And we could really use the space."

"No worries. I'll be out of your hair in a minute."

"Thank you. Really." She glanced over her shoulder again. "And I apologize if Dr. Astell was rude." She chuckled. "I'm afraid he's not known for his bedside manner, although as an oracle, he's excellent at triage."

She ducked back, but before she could close the curtain, I asked, "If you don't mind an impertinent question, what is your supe nature?"

She grinned, a little toothily. "Werewolf."

"Awesome," I said. "Our junior investigator is a were, too."

"Oh, Jordan." She chuckled. "We see him so often, he's practically got his own suite. Tell him hello from Renee, okay?"

"Will do."

After she left, I pulled on my jeans, wincing because still no underwear. I wonder what the ER staff thought about that. Weren't you always supposed to wear clean underwear in case you were in an accident? I never understood that part. Were medical personnel especially judgy about undergarments?

I grimaced when I held up my shirt. It was soaked with blood from the ragged gash all the way to the hem. "Well, this is toast."

Then I caught sight of Lachlan's face through the gap. He looked absolutely wrecked, his eyes locked on that bloodstain. I tossed the shirt aside and launched myself at him, hugging him tight around the waist. "Oh, sweetheart. Please don't look like that. I'm fine."

"Matthew," he said as he enveloped me in a nearly smothering hug. "Please say you'll swim with me."

"We'll talk about that later, okay?" I pulled back and kissed him. "But right now, I've got an appointment with Death. Join me?"

He nodded and took my hand. I begged a scrub shirt from a passing orderly and we headed out to catch an Uber.

But when we got back to the Quest offices, Yannick Tan was gone.

CHAPTER EIGHT

"Great. Just great." I frowned at the empty conference room. I suppose I couldn't really be surprised—between Ronnie's accident, my injury, and my stint at St. Stupid's, it had been at least two hours. Even Death can't wait around forever.

Lachlan put a hand on my shoulder. "Matthew. Don't you think you should go home? Rest?"

I leaned into his touch, because despite still being seriously irritated about the broom ambush, that wasn't really Lachlan's fault. At least, I didn't think it was. He wasn't the kind of guy who did sneaky very well—he was much too direct. Witness his behavior at the hospital.

"I feel fine, which you should know perfectly well. David's healed your injuries before, too." I looked up at him, lifting my eyebrows. "As I recall, you didn't rest quietly after he'd finished with you, either." Soon after we first met, Lachlan had been mugged and ended up at St. Stupid's himself.

He scowled. "That was different."

"Oh, really?" I drawled. "Because you're a big strong supe and I'm a lowly human?"

The scowl deepened. "No. Because you— Because I— Because we—"

"Yes? Go on."

"Just because."

"Brilliant logic, Lachlan." I sighed and collected my notepad. Yannick's plate and the Van Gogh tea pot on its tray were still on the table, which was odd. Zeke usually cleaned up after client meetings before any of us could blink—demon super-speed was a thing. For Zeke, at any rate, not globally, since demons were all purpose-built by their progenitors. That thought made *me* scowl—just another instance of supe power brokers depriving lower status folk of choice. AJ, the demon who did diagnostic possessions for St. Stupid's, for instance, couldn't interact with fire at all, not even contained flames like a stove burner. Weird, right, since Sheol is kind of the definition of a fiery pit, at least in some spots. But AJ's progenitor manifested him as a library assistant, and the jerkface didn't want there to be any chance that AJ could damage his books.

As Mal would say, *that wanker.*

"Matthew. Can we talk about this morning? I know you're still a wee bit fashed by the besom jumping—"

"You think?"

"I'd never want to rush you. But now that the deed is done..." He ducked his head and peered up at me from under his brows. "Is it really so bad?"

I sighed heavily. "That's not the point, Lachlan. You supes have millennia of history of *not asking permission*. In this, you're as much a victim as I am. The selkies ambushed you as well as me. I mean, what gave them the idea that *you* wanted to be shackled to someone else when you'd only been technically *un*shackled for mere weeks?"

Even beneath his tan, I could spot the flush on his cheeks. "I...may have mentioned you to them. Once or twice."

"Once or twice?"

"Perhaps more," he muttered. "Along with my hopes." He lifted his chin and met my gaze. "But only so they would stand down, stop pressuring me. One thing that's always been sacred to selkies is the courtship with our human mates. I thought that would get them to give me—give us—more time."

There was that word again: *mate*. I was pretty sure Lachlan didn't mean it the way Mal did—meaning *friend* rather than *life partner, significant other*, or, you know, *husband*. I might have had dreams of getting there with Lachlan one day, but only when one of us actually *asked* the other and got an affirmative in response.

"Look, there's a lot we have to unpack about this morning, but given that I've got Slacker Death threatening me with..." Come to think of it, I hadn't really studied the lawsuit, so I wasn't sure what kind of damages Yannick intended to wring from me. Whatever it was, I doubted it would be anything good. "So can we table the discussion for a while? If we—"

A sound penetrated the room. At first I thought it was the whine of a power tool, although it seemed unlikely that the supe equivalent of OSHA would have finished with the evaluation of the accident site already. Then I realized the whine was animal, not machine.

"That's Doop." I tossed the pad back on the table—it was blank anyway, since I hadn't had a chance to take any notes—and headed for the door.

"Matthew, wait." For a change, Lachlan's tone was soft, almost cajoling. "Cannot you spare me a few minutes?"

I glanced back at him—he wasn't scowling, which was weird enough, but if Doop was whining, all wasn't right with Jordan's world. "I will, Lachlan. I promise. But this is my job."

"As my consort—"

"Not. Now." I growled. I wasn't about to leave Quest to become Lachlan's house husband or princess or whatever. Yeah, we needed to talk, but right now, my team needed me more. I paused by the door. "Coming?"

His expression cleared. "For you? Always."

I tried not to assign any double entendres to that and barreled down the stairs with Lachlan pounding close behind. When I rushed into the lobby, Doop was attempting to hide under one of the cushy client chairs. However, since he was approximately the size of a MINI Cooper, he'd only succeeded in cramming his head underneath, lifting it off its legs. His body and tail—currently tucked so close to his behind that he probably had a cramp—stretched halfway across the room.

Jordan was crouched next to him, stroking the hound's fluffy white fur. "It's okay, boy. I'm here." Doop whined again, and Jordan sighed. "Sometimes I wish you could talk. It would be so much easier to figure out what you really want."

"Hellhound chatter," Eleri muttered. "That's all we need." She was standing against the wall behind Zeke's desk, her arms tight across her middle, and if I didn't know my BFF better, I'd say she was completely terrified. But Eleri didn't do terrified—she was one of the most fearless people I knew. Case in point: She, a dryad, spent months serving as a maid in a *fire mage's* house. Plus, she was one of the cadre of dryads who'd stood up to the outdated policies of the old dryad leadership.

Of Zeke, there was no sign.

Crap. Had he gotten injured in the Ronnie woodpile incident, too?

"What's going on, guys?" I asked. "Where's Zeke?"

Doop's tail thumped once before it resumed its butt-clench. Jordan jumped to his feet. "Hugh!" He leaped over Doop's back to hug me. "You're okay!" He retreated a step, glancing from me to Lachlan. "I mean, you *are* okay, right?"

I nodded. "Never better."

"Somehow, I doubt that," Eleri said as Jordan dropped down next to Doop again and recommenced the comfort stroking. "Hello? Close encounter with a saw blade? What the hell, Hugh?" Her gaze cut to the desk again, where a pencil rolled off the blotter and onto the floor.

"I'm fine. But you didn't answer my question. Where's Zeke? He wasn't hurt, was he?"

Eleri shook her head as another pencil joined the first on the carpet. "He's okay, but when he tried to come back to work, Hamish roared in and spirited him away. Apparently, he has definite opinions about Zeke spending any time in his old apartment space." She shrugged. "Feelings. What can you do?"

I frowned. "But Zeke didn't seem upset about being up there. Other than Ronnie's accident, I mean."

"Not *Zeke's* feelings. *Hamish's* feelings," she said, with a sly glance at Lachlan. "You know how freaked out some people get when their essos are in danger."

"Essos?" I said.

"You know." She made a dismissive gesture with one hand as a third pencil rolled off the desk—and seriously, what was going on with that? Had the construction somehow compromised the building's structure? "Significant others. SOs. Essos."

"Ah. Got it." A fourth pencil rolled across the blotter. "What's with the pencils, anyway?"

"That's what's upsetting Doop," Jordan said.

"He objects to pencils? I know they're not Frisbees, but—"

"Not the pencils, per se," Eleri said. "What's *moving* the pencils."

My chest tightened, and I reached for Lachlan's hand. "Th-they're not just responding to gravity?"

"Nope." As soon as she said that, Zeke's stapler fell onto its side. "Apparently Zeke's desk is haunted. Or maybe possessed."

"Haunted?" Zeke's recent words about untethered souls came back to me, and I suspected that *haunted* wasn't precisely the right word. "Hold that thought." I dropped Lachlan's hand.

"Matthew?"

"I'll be back in a minute." I kissed him quickly. "Promise."

I raced out of the lobby and up the stairs to my office. My camera bag wasn't on the shelf beside my desk where I always kept it. "Where—" Oh. Right. I'd taken it to the conference room for the meeting with Yannick. I took a quick detour to collect it, then ran back to the lobby.

I set my bag down as far away from the haunted-slash-possessed desk as possible, since I didn't especially want it to join the pencils in their dive to the floor. It was padded, sure, but some of my equipment was irreplaceable—like, for instance, the telephoto lens that allowed me to see…unseen things.

I lifted the camera out and switched the 50mm lens for the magical one. I took a deep breath, because I wasn't entirely sure what—or rather who—I'd see. I raised the camera and peered through the viewfinder, panning to check out the entire room.

I exhaled shakily. I'd been half afraid that the lobby would be crowded with untethered souls, all on the trail of Yannick Tan and their ticket onward. But the only noncorporeal entity sat straight-backed in Zeke's chair, an expression of stern disapproval on the thin face under a black straw hat with a turned-up brim and a single feather quivering over its low crown.

Furthermore, I recognized her. I'd seen her in the Sheol Reception and Disposal room, and had mentally dubbed her Victorian Suffragette. The bustle on her high-necked gray gown wasn't visible—I spared a moment to wonder how that worked with Zeke's Aeron chair—and the lower half of the sash draped over her shoulder was hidden by the desk, so it only read *Votes for W.* But it was definitely the same person. Soul. Entity. Whatever.

I pressed the shutter, since nobody else could see what I saw unless I actually captured the shot. "Good afternoon, ma'am. Welcome to Quest Investigations. How may we assist you?"

CHAPTER NINE

Victorian Suffragette's lips moved, but I couldn't hear anything. Her expression reminded me of my eighth-grade algebra teacher, right before she'd handed the whole class detention for goofing off during a lesson on binomials.

Jordan and Eleri both stared at me, wide-eyed. Lachlan, of course, growled. Doop whined.

Eleri held up a palm between her and the chair and jabbed a finger at it, as though she were hiding the gesture from Victorian Suffragette. "Is there somebody there?" she whispered.

Victorian Suffragette shot her a disgusted look, accompanied by an obviously disdainful sniff.

"Yep. And she can hear you, so there's no point in trying to be sneaky."

"Shit," she muttered. "Sorry, er"—she glanced at me—"ma'am?"

"No wonder Doop is so upset," Jordan fretted. "Hector told a ghost story over pizza last week, and Doop hid under my bed all night."

"She's not a ghost." I kept my eye on Victorian Suffragette. "She's what Zeke calls an untethered soul." She nodded with apparent approval. "I think she might be looking for Yannick." She scowled at that. "Or maybe not." She folded her hands on the desk—I could see the blotter through her transparent flesh—

and fixed me with an expectant look. "If it's all right with you, ma'am, I'd like to show your...your image to my associates."

When she nodded graciously, I showed the photo first to Lachlan, then to Eleri, and last to Jordan.

"Wow." Jordan cast a sidelong glance at Doop. "Do you think you could show that to him? If he'll come out from under the chair, that is?"

"I suspect he can probably see her on his own. You know—H-word?"

"Oh. Right." Jordan sighed. "I guess that makes sense, but I wish he wasn't so scared."

I tried to be subtle about pointing the camera toward Victorian Suffragette, but from the lift of her eyebrow, I wasn't successful. I wished Zeke were here. I mean, yeah, he wasn't originally rated for soul collection, and he hadn't been able to see the souls in Sheol Reception and Disposal, which had looked more like a 1940s newsroom than an antechamber to hell. But as a demon, he'd have a better chance than the rest of us to—

Wait. The souls in Reception and Disposal had been configured to handle clerical tasks. Victorian Suffragette herself had been typing on a manual typewriter. She'd flicked pencils off Zeke's desk, so she could affect Upper World environment to some extent, too.

We didn't have a manual typewriter, but we had Zeke's computer.

I sidled around the desk, hoping I wasn't about to get Zeke's whole system fried from supernatural etheric energy, or whatever. "Ma'am, I know you're a very efficient typist, and while we don't have the kind of equipment you're accustomed to, this keyboard functions very similarly."

I slid the keyboard toward me and pulled up a simple text app. Then I typed, *My name is Hugh. What's yours?*

I pointed to the screen, and then pushed the keyboard so it was directly in front of the chair. Since I wasn't looking through the lens, I hoped I hadn't just shoved it through her hands.

For a moment, nothing happened. Then the keyboard began to click, its keys depressing, slowly at first, but then more quickly as she got accustomed to its touch. Eleri sidled closer, although Jordan stayed on the floor next to Doop, who continued to whimper.

You may call me Miss Pennybaker.

Okay, then. "Miss Pennybaker. May I ask why you've chosen to, er, honor us with a visit?

I assumed your establishment would be more well-run than hell. Clearly I was mistaken.

Great. Not only untethered souls, but *judgmental* untethered souls. I shared a glance with Eleri. "You're, um, not exactly seeing us at our best."

The cursor simply blinked in place. Apparently, Miss Pennybaker didn't consider that statement worthy of a response.

Before I could figure out what else to ask, voices echoed in the stairwell. One of them was unmistakably Zeke's light tenor, its tone placating. The other was deeper, and even though I couldn't make out the words, I assumed, given Zeke's quick response, that the other person wasn't pleased.

"Uh oh," Jordan murmured. "Hamish *really* doesn't want Zeke to come back here."

"You can understand what they're saying?" I asked.

Eleri nudged me. "Werewolf hearing, remember?"

"Oh. Right." Werewolves could both smell and hear more keenly than humans. I tapped my fingers against the seam of my jeans. Encouraging Jordan to eavesdrop on a colleague would be bad. I shouldn't encourage it, right? I should take the high road. I should— Ah, screw it. "What's Hamish's concern?"

"Matthew." Lachlan's tone—not to mention the way he crossed his arms over his chest—telegraphed his disapproval.

But what can I say? I'm not the best role model when it comes to discretion. Too many years spent scrounging for the least scrap of information that would lead me to a cryptid sighting, and hey, we're a private investigation firm. It's our job to snoop. So I ignored him.

Jordan frowned in concentration. "He—that is Hamish—says Zeke should stay home until the renovations are done. That he's never been happy about Zeke working in the same building as when he was still a Sheol minion. That he doesn't have to work at all, since Hamish has enough money for both of them."

The keyboard clacked again. *No demon may remain in the Upper World without gainful employment.*

"They're not called demons anymore, you know." Although I'd been guilty of referring to Zeke and AJ that way myself. I made a mental note to try to be more inclusive. "They're simply part of the Host."

Semantics, Miss Pennybaker typed.

I huffed a sigh. She had a point. Even though the entities formerly known as demons were now part of the larger group that included former angels as well, the demonic Host were saddled with a lot more restrictions than the angelic Host, which didn't seem fair to me at all. The worst behaved member of the Host I'd ever encountered had been an angel—a fact he'd never let anybody forget, until Herne had dispatched him along with his demon co-conspirator.

Chalk that up to yet another supe policy in need of reform. I was keeping a list. It wasn't short.

Zeke appeared in the archway that led to the landing, his big blond kangaroo shifter boyfriend—or should I adopt Eleri's verbiage and call him an *esso?*—at his side, an arm draped protectively over Zeke's shoulders.

Zeke gazed up at Hamish with obvious affection. "I'll be fine, my Orpheus. Now go. The band is waiting for you in the recording studio."

Hamish's scowl held more worry than anger, but he shook his head and drew Zeke in for a kiss that bordered on NSFW. "All right. But if you're not home by seven, I'm coming back to collect you."

Zeke smiled at him and kissed his cheek. "Sounds like I win either way." He stayed on the landing, watching Hamish tromp down the stairs, and uttered a small sigh when the outside door *whump*ed closed. When he turned and saw all of us watching him, his blotchy blush painted his skin. "Oh. Hello."

"If you'll pardon me," Lachlan said, "I'll just have a word with Hamish."

Zeke watched him go, but when he turned back, his gaze landed on me. "Hugh!" He rushed over, gaze traveling over me as if he were checking for remaining wounds. "Oh my stars, I was so worried."

"I'm fine." I patted my side. Jeez, I was still wearing scrubs. So not attractive, but I didn't have another spare shirt at the office. "David patched me right up."

Zeke bit his lip. "I truly appreciate your efforts, but it wasn't necessary. That saw couldn't have hurt me. Not permanently, anyway."

"I'll keep that in mind for our next brush with death and dismemberment." I winced, remembering that I hadn't entirely evaded my brush with death-with-a-capital-D.

Zeke's brow puckered as he studied Eleri and me standing beside his seemingly vacant chair, at Jordan planted on the floor, and at the whimpering hellhound with his head under a chair. "Is...something going on?"

I couldn't help it. I laughed. "You could say that." I gestured to the chair. "Zeke, meet Miss Pennybaker, formerly of Sheol Reception and Disposal."

His eyes behind his glasses grew round and his lips parted in a soft *oooh*. Then he blushed so hard he looked like a monochrome Twister mat. "Madam, if I ever encountered you in Sheol and did *anything* that distressed you, let me assure you that it wasn't my intent."

I raised my eyebrows. "Could you see any of them back then? While you were still trapped there?"

Zeke shook his head. "No. Any souls I interacted with"—his blush spread—"were invisible to me, although not insubstantial."

The keyboard clacked again. We all leaned toward the monitor, although Zeke had to crane his neck at an awkward angle.

Votes for Minions.

Eleri chuckled. "That looks like a statement of solidarity to me, Zeke."

"Although not precisely an acceptance of my apology," he muttered miserably.

More keyboard clacking. *Don't cringe, young man. Dog biscuit.*

Zeke blinked. "Did she just call me a dog biscuit?"

"No," I said, "I think she's asking for one. Jordan?"

He stopped murmuring to Doop and looked up. "Yes, Hugh?"

"Have you got any dog treats at hand?"

"Oh, sure. Several kinds, because sometimes Doop's in the mood for carbs, but other times he needs protein, you know?"

"Could you dig one out for Miss Pennybaker? I think she's got something in mind that might spring Doop from time-out."

He nodded and patted Doop's back. "I'll be right back, boy. Don't worry." He scrambled to his feet and collected the oversized pack dubbed the Dooper bag by Eleri. He'd begun carting it around with him everywhere after he'd become Doop's official...not master. Guardian? Caretaker? Partner in crime? I wasn't entirely sure what to call their relationship, but it seemed to work for both of them.

After rummaging in it, he extracted a palm-sized biscuit that looked as though it were made from oatmeal and twigs. "He likes these when he's feeling stressed, so I think it's the best choice." He glanced between me, Eleri, Zeke, and the empty chair. "Um…"

Miss Pennybaker gave the keyboard another workout. *Hold it out politely, you ridiculous boy. And inform your hound that if he does not wish to be reprimanded, he must keep his paws off the furniture.*

Jordan flushed as he followed instructions. "When we got here, Doop propped himself on Zeke's desk like normal. He's always so excited to see you, even when you're not here." The treat left Jordan's hand and seemed to float in the air for a moment. Jordan winced and pressed his fingers behind his ears. "Do you hear that whistle?"

"Nope," Eleri said.

I said, "Me neither."

Doop, apparently, didn't have that problem, because he inched backward until he could turn and slink toward the desk. Eleri grinned. "I guess it's one of those sounds that only dogs can hear, eh, Jordan?"

He cast her a resigned glance as Doop rose slowly to all four legs. At his full height, he was able to stretch his neck out and delicately take the treat in his very impressive jaws. He backed away and dropped to his belly in the corner to munch on it, but seemed more or less contented.

"I guess he wasn't afraid of Miss Pennybaker's presence," I said, "only responding to a *bad dog* message."

Jordan's expression turned serious, and he faced Miss Pennybaker's spot. "I'm sorry Doop misbehaved, but if you don't mind, I'd rather not use words with him like *bad*. He's still young, still being trained, so I don't want to send him any mixed messages, or make it seem like it's him personally and not a particular behavior that's the problem." He lowered his voice, glancing briefly over his shoulder at Doop. "Positive reinforcement is *very* important."

There was no response from Miss Pennybaker. I hoped that meant she accepted Jordan's request. Jordan didn't get militant often, but a threat to Doop was a sure way to bring out his alpha side.

Lachlan slipped back into the room and gave me a *come hither* glance—*come hither* as in *come over here* as opposed to *let me jump your bones*. Unfortunately.

I walked over to his spot near the door. "Everything okay?"

"Aye. I just let Hamish know I'd keep an eye on Zeke for him."

"Did that make him feel better?"

Lachlan chuckled, his dark eyes as merry as I'd ever seen them. "Nay. He told me to keep my eyes to myself or on my own boyfriend." His expression dimmed. "You needn't worry, *mo cridhe*. I didn't tell him you're my—"

"Don't say it." I glanced over my shoulder at my team. "Not yet, and definitely not here."

"Matthew—"

Luckily for me, Quest's incoming line rang, or I'd have crumpled under the hurt in Lachlan's gaze. Zeke reached to answer the phone but missed because the handset rose into the air to hover near—presumably—Miss Pennybaker's ear. We could all hear someone on the other end of the call saying, "Hello? Hello? Is this Quest Investigations? Is anybody there?"

Zeke cleared his throat. "I don't believe the calling party can hear you, madam, so if you don't mind, may I have the receiver?"

There was a slight pause, accompanied by another *Hello?* from the caller, then the handset flew toward Zeke.

He caught it neatly. "Quest Investigations. This is Zeke. How may I help you?" His brows pinched together and he glanced at me. "Yes, he's here. Would you like to— Oh. All right. I'll let him know. Thank you." He hung up. "That was the ER charge nurse at St. Stupid's."

I raised my own eyebrows. "Renee?"

"Yes. She asked if you could return to the hospital."

"I knew they let you go too early," Lachlan growled.

Zeke held up a placating hand. "It has nothing to do with your treatment, Hugh, don't worry. She said that Ronnie Purl is awake and asking for you."

I frowned. "Ronnie? Why? He was barely conscious when the saw nicked me, so I don't blame him, and it's not like we're buddies."

Zeke shrugged. "She said he was quite agitated and insistent. No pressure, of course, but she wondered if, as a favor, you could speak with him. She thinks it might help settle him."

I'd learned over my time with Quest not to pass up a chance to cultivate connections in the community. You never knew when you might need to call on them for information. "I don't mind."

"Matthew," Lachlan growled. "You owe him nothing."

I propped my fists on my hips and narrowed my eyes. "Don't tell me *you* blame him?"

He folded his arms. "I have to blame somebody."

"No you don't. Sometimes an accident is just an accident." When he simply grunted, I sighed and gripped his forearm. "What's really the matter?"

"Nothing," he muttered.

"Lachlan." I loaded my tone with a ton of *don't-give-me-that*. "Tell me." He muttered something I couldn't hear. "What was that?"

He lifted his head, his expression rivaling Doop's when he faced Miss Pennybaker. "I hate hospitals, all right?"

I didn't laugh, because it had clearly cost him to admit his discomfort. I laid my hands on his chest and he covered them with his own. "You don't have to go with me if it makes you uncomfortable."

"Somebody should."

"Tine. Eleri can—"

"Sorry, Hugh," she said. "Jordan and I have that theft case. We've got a lead on the stolen items and as soon as Doop"—she glanced at the dog, who'd finished his treat and had laid his head on his paws, although he kept his eyes focused on the desk —"recovers, we've got to head back out."

"No worries." I faced Lachlan again. "All I'm doing is visiting a patient. I don't really need an escort. I'll be fine." I kissed him, because that was a thing I could do now, even without the accidental mating ceremony. "They'll probably welcome me more warmly if you're *not* with me, considering the fuss you made last time."

He smiled crookedly. "Aye. Perhaps you're right." He kissed my forehead and then my lips. "Besides, I have some business to take care of with the bloody selkies." He grimaced. "Best handle that now as later."

"You might gift them with a dictionary and mark the page with the definition of *consent*. Know what I'm saying?"

He chuckled. "Aye." He kissed me again. "Call me when you get home?"

"Absolutely."

I waited in the archway as he headed up the stairs, presumably to our dimensional portal where he could call an FTA driver to get him back to the boat—or maybe to take him to Scotland to harangue the selkie clan leadership face to face.

"Hugh?" Jordan said quietly. "It shouldn't take us long to finish the case. We can join you at the hospital afterward if you want."

I smiled down at him where he was sitting cross-legged, his fingers buried in Doop's ruff. "No. I really don't need anyone to hold my hand. It's a hospital, for Pete's sake. What could happen?"

CHAPTER
TEN

Turns out, a lot could happen in a hospital, but not, thank goodness, to me.

When I stepped into the ER, a gray *something* flew directly at my head. I ducked, but the gray object squawked, "Sorry!"

I realized, as the object flapped toward a familiar-looking man in an SMT uniform, that it was a parrot, and that I'd seen both of them before. The SMT—Ky, that was his name—and his partner had taken the call when we'd found Reid Martinson face down in the Nehalem River. The parrot, if I recalled correctly, was Zuri, and she was his familiar. Which made him a witch. I had mixed feelings about witches in general, since some of them had treated Zeke and Ted poorly—*understatement*—in the past. Consequently, I hadn't spent much effort stalking—as Eleri would say, but I preferred to think of it as *interviewing*— any witches to find out how they fit into the supernatural community. Maybe it was time to let go of that prejudice and follow up with some of them.

Zuri wheeled and squawked while Ky and his partner—Pete? —worked over a patient stretched on a gurney, so I decided now wasn't the best time to approach them.

Renee hurried by, a clipboard under one arm. "Renee? Hi, you asked me to come in."

She blinked at me, clearly trying to place me and remember why she could possibly have asked me to come in.

"I'm Hugh Mann. You wanted me to speak with Ronnie Purl?"

She shook her head, but more to clear it than to say no. "Hugh. Of course. I'm sorry. Things have gotten a bit chaotic here since you were discharged."

I backed up to get out of the way when David hurried past, accompanied by a taller man with sandy brown hair. *Ky's partner*. The *other* kind of partner. "Is that Ewan Jones?"

She nodded. "Yes. We've had to call in Ewan and his sister to assist David."

I frowned. "They're all *achubyddion*, right? I thought they only consulted on critical cases." Or when their friends called in a favor. I tried not to cringe because David had wasted time and energy on my relatively minor injury.

"Ordinarily, yes." Another nurse rushed over to her and she handed him the clipboard. "But for some reason, Dr. Astell has barricaded himself in his office and is refusing to treat any patients. We've had to ask the *achubyddion* triage team to step in until we can either get Dr. Astell to re-engage or get another on-call physician in to cover his shift."

I frowned. "Does Dr. Astell frequently refuse to treat patients?"

"No. Never." She winced, no doubt remembering that he'd refused to treat me. "That is, almost never. We've had a sudden influx of patients this evening, and though none of them have been serious so far—first-degree burns, cuts, a broken bone or two, near alcohol poisonings—there have been a *lot* of them."

Ky and Pete pushed their gurney into a bay that had just been cleared by an orderly, Zuri mantling her wings as she tried to maintain her balance on Ky's shoulder.

"Look," I said, as I dodged a nurse hurrying past with an IV stand, "I don't want to get in the way. If you could just point me to Ronnie—"

"Oh. I'm so sorry." She brushed back a lock of salt-and-pepper hair that had come loose from her hair clip. "I should have called back. Ronnie's been discharged already. After Dr. Astell retreated into his inner sanctum"—she rolled her eyes— "David and Ewan treated his injuries. Healed him completely. Since we needed the space, we pushed his discharge paperwork through. His brother took him up to the business office to clear up some insurance questions." She bit her lip. "I really am sorry, Hugh. I didn't mean to waste your time."

"No worries. I'll just—"

The ER doors swung open again. My jaw dropped because this time, the SMTs were accompanied by Jordan and Eleri. Jordan spotted me. "Hugh!" he called, his voice cutting through ER cacophony. Since Renee was done with me, I trotted over to meet him.

"What's going on?" I asked as Eleri joined us, leaving the SMTs conferring in that incomprehensible staccato ER shorthand common to medical personnel in both supe and human hospitals. "I thought you guys were tracking down stolen objects."

"We were," she said. "We did. But we didn't exactly find what we expected."

I nodded at the person on the gurney. "Is that the alleged thief?"

"No." She shook her head. "Nor is he the victim."

"Then what—"

"He ran out in front of a car," Jordan said with a grimace. "And since that happened to me once, I know what it's like. We called the SMTs, but the guy was so freaked out that we didn't want to leave."

I peered around, checking for hippo-sized canines. "Where's Doop?"

Jordan gave me a severe look. "Really, Hugh. I couldn't bring him into an *emergency room.*"

"Ah. Right. Good point." While the staff might often treat shifters who'd morphed into their animal nature, they didn't treat actual animals, no matter how uncanny.

"Imagine how upset he'd be," Jordan said.

I shared an amused glance with Eleri. "Wouldn't want that, now, would we?" I gestured to the doors leading to the waiting room. "Let's get out of the way, shall we? You can fill me in on the case when we're not underfoot."

We trooped through the doors and settled into a trio of orange plastic chairs. I could understand why an ER might stock furnishings that were easy to clean, but did they always have to be so dang uncomfortable?

"Okay," I said. "What's the story with your theft case?"

Eleri chuckled. "Turns out we solved not just our case, but some that were never reported. We found a cache of jewelry—"

"And those big rubber rods," Jordan put in. "Don't forget those."

"Yes, jewelry and"—she cut a glance at Jordan—"some adult entertainment items."

Jordan blinked at her. "Is *that* what those were? I had no *idea* they came in that size."

"Yes. Well." Eleri cleared her throat, clearly trying not to laugh. "Anyway, it was like a magpie's nest, full of random treasures, as if the thief—"

"Or thieves," Jordan said. "There were definitely several scents. Doop and I both picked up on them. But we didn't have a chance to track them back to their sources before that poor guy got hit by the car."

I frowned. "Was it a hit and run? Did you catch the driver?"

"Oh, the driver didn't flee the scene. She was devastated. In fact, she refused to leave, which was a big problem once we realized the victim was a supe."

Jordan nodded. "Bobcat shifter."

"So I made a quick call to Mal, and he showed up to blind the driver with fae *glamourie*." Eleri chuckled. "She's totally convinced that she made the appropriate police reports, and that *somehow* her car wasn't damaged in the least."

"Was it? Damaged, I mean?"

She nodded. "Yes. But I don't imagine it will be for long. Mal said he'd send along a team of gnome metalworkers. They'll repair it before the *glamourie* wears off."

"And Zeke will send her the police report thingy," Jordan said, "so she'll be fine."

"As long as she's not traumatized by hitting somebody with her car."

"Oh, she wasn't going fast at all, and the bobcat guy darted out with no warning." Jordan scrunched up his nose. "If she does have a problem, Mal gave her Dr. Kendrick's number too, so, you know, psychology— Oh, hey, Wash! Hi, AJ!" Jordan waved at the two men in hospital scrubs who were powering toward the ER. "Busy night?"

The two of them raised their hands in greeting and gave Jordan somewhat distracted smiles before disappearing through the doors. AJ was the demon who did diagnostic possessions and Wash was his boyfriend, a witch who'd unexpectedly bonded with AJ as a familiar, something that had never happened before. Now, those two would merit a whole series of interviews. I wondered if Zeke could set it up for me—he and AJ were friends, after all.

"Hey, if I asked Dr. Kendrick, would he—"

A shout, a scream, and a crash interrupted Jordan's words. All three of us jumped to our feet as several other hospital personnel rushed past, including Dr. Mori, a kitsune who was the head of diagnostic medicine.

"What do you— Jordan!" Eleri grabbed for Jordan, but werewolves were *fast*. He darted through the ER doors, leaving her grasping the air. "Goddess," she muttered, "we can't let him blunder around in there. We'd better go get him."

"Are you kidding? At this rate, it's probably standing room only. It'll be like the stateroom scene in *A Night at the Opera*."

She frowned at me. "What?"

"Never mind." I grabbed her elbow. "Let's get him and tow him out before they ban him for life. He's way too accident prone to be barred from the ER."

I eased the door open and we slipped inside. I'd like to claim we totally rocked an unobtrusive entrance, but we could probably have marched in with an entire brass band and nobody would have noticed. I didn't see Jordan anywhere—maybe he was in one of the curtained bays—but a figure in a white lab coat was sprawled face down on the floor.

"Is that Dr. Asshole?" Eleri murmured.

"I think so," I replied.

Ky was kneeling next to him, Zuri flapping agitatedly on his shoulder. All eight of Dr. Mori's tails swished under her lab coat as she frowned down at the body. AJ's wings were out—which gave me a jolt since they were as vast and leathery as Quentin's wings, which were my first in-your-face proof not only that supes existed, but that Ted Farnsworth was out of my reach. But AJ's wings weren't spread—a good thing, since his wingspan was easily over twelve feet. Instead they were curved around Wash, who was sagging in his boyfriend's embrace.

Eleri and I kept out of the way, backs against the door. Yeah, we probably should have cleared out and let the staff do their work, but Jordan was in here somewhere, in close proximity to many sharp implements. Leaving was more hazardous—at least for Jordan—than staying.

"Turn him over, please, Mr. Hernandez," Dr. Mori said.

Ky slipped one arm under Dr. Asshole—*Dr. Astell*—and levered him onto his back. My belly jolted, and beside me, Eleri gulped. Because the staring eyes, the slack jaw, the pallid skin? I didn't need Ky's grim expression or the slight shake of his head to know the score.

Dr. Asshole was undeniably dead.

CHAPTER
ELEVEN

I expected Dr. Mori to order Eleri and me to get the hell out, but she didn't even glance at us. "Gurney. Now," she snapped at a goggling orderly.

He jumped to comply—and heck, I'd have done the same if she'd used that tone on me. I wasn't certain she still wouldn't once she noticed us. With the orderly's help, Ky and Pete lifted Dr. Astell's body onto the gurney.

"Where do you want him, Doctor?" Ky asked.

"The diagnostics lab." She turned in a flare of white coat and fox tails, and *then* she saw us. "Unless you're a family member of someone here in the ER, leave. Immediately."

"No, Dr. Mori," AJ said, his deep voice trembling. "We'll need their help."

She glanced at him sharply. "Their help? Why? They're not medical personnel."

"No," he said, "but they're with Quest, and we'll need their services."

I straightened up at that, attempting to look competent and professional instead of barely off an ER gurney myself. Heck, was I still wearing the borrowed scrub shirt, a few grains of sand were abrading some rather sensitive places, and my skin was still itchy from salt water immersion. "We're here to help. Whatever you need."

"Absolutely," Eleri said.

Dr. Mori fixed us with a narrow-eyed glare that I was surprised didn't pin us to the wall. "Are you certain, AJ?"

He nodded miserably. "Yes."

"Why?"

"Because…because somebody just tried to possess Wash."

Well, *that* got everyone's attention. Her gaze snapped to him and then to us. "Very well. Diagnostics. Now. All of you."

In an attempt to be marginally useful, I pushed the doors open so Ky and Pete could wheel Dr. Astell's sheet-covered body through.

"The doors are automatic, Hugh," Eleri murmured. "Get with the program."

Her words might hold the usual Eleri attitude, but her tone? Yeah, she was just as shaken as I was.

"What about Jordan?"

"We'll have to collect him later. The ER staff can probably keep him contained. They've had plenty of practice."

We fell in behind Wash and AJ, the caboose at the end of the sad little train.

I'd never been to the St. Stupid's diagnostics lab. Ordinarily I'd be cataloging everything mentally so I could add my impressions to my notes later, but for some reason, I couldn't tear my gaze away from the way Wash nestled under AJ's arm, or the way AJ's wings still wrapped around him.

Clearly, AJ and Wash depended on each other. Their relationship wasn't one-sided, with all the power in one court. I had zero doubts that if AJ were ill or in trouble, Wash would tuck him against his side just as tightly, although probably without the wings.

It made me long for Lachlan.

Stupid? Maybe. Pathetic? Definitely. But that kind of mutual comfort and support was what I craved, even more than sex. I'd probably made a huge mistake sending him away.

Twenty-twenty hindsight, and all that.

We all crowded into the elevator. After Dr. Mori punched the button for the third floor, she looked at me again, which made me back up a step and run into Eleri. She uttered an *oof* and elbowed me in the ribs. That made me wince because she'd hit the exact spot where Ronnie had filleted me.

Eleri caught my wince. "Oh, Goddess, Hugh, I'm sorry."

"It's okay," I said, a little breathlessly.

Dr. Mori caught the interaction. "Are you well? Mister... Mann, is it?"

"Yeah. Fine. Just had my own ER stint a little earlier."

She replied with a noncommittal hum. "So why return now? Had you forgotten something?"

"No." The elevator pinged and the doors slid open. We spilled out into a small waiting area. "Renee called because apparently the guy who'd accidentally injured me was awake and asking to speak to me." I shrugged. "When I got here, though, he'd apparently changed his mind."

She shifted her laser-gaze to Eleri. "And you chose to accompany him?"

"N-no." She shot a wild-eyed glance at me—Dr. Mori had that effect on everybody, it seemed. "Jordan Tate and I accompanied a hit-and-run victim."

"Were you the driver who struck this victim?" Wow, if I thought the doctor was scary before, I needed to recalibrate my scary scale, because, *yikes.*

"No! We were witnesses."

"Then I don't understand why you're here. Surely the SMTs on the scene could manage without your assistance."

"Of course they could. But...but..." Her brow wrinkled. "You know, I'm not entirely sure *why* we came, only Jordan wanted to make sure the guy was all right and Mal—Mal Kendrick, our boss—probably wanted to get us out of the way so he could handle damage control with the human driver."

With another noncommittal hum, Dr. Mori led the way into a room the size of one of the Quest workrooms, tricked out in a combination of tech and—if the wrist-thick candles, both black and white, atop tall wrought-iron stands in the corners were any indication—magic. Ky and Pete wheeled Dr. Astell's body to the center of the room under a bank of lights and locked the wheels in place.

"Do you need us for anything else, Doctor?" Ky asked.

She shook her head, her shiny black hair settling back perfectly into its smooth cap. "No. Thank you, Mr. Hernandez, Mr. Cotton. You may return to your duties. Although"—with a single word, she stopped them in their tracks—"should anything else…unusual…occur on your shift, please inform me at once."

"Of course," Ky said, and although Pete left immediately, Ky detoured to grip Wash's shoulder and murmur something in his ear. *Oh, right. They're brothers. I forgot.* Then he exited, Zuri winging out ahead of him.

Dr. Mori sat behind a desk, pushed one of her triple monitors aside, and folded her hands next to the keyboard. She nodded at the chairs arranged in front of it. "If you could all join me, please."

Eleri and I hustled to obey, and I gave brief thanks that the lab rated cushioned chairs with actual armrests rather than the ER's orange plastic monstrosities. AJ led Wash over more slowly.

Wash glanced at him a little irritably. "I'm not made of glass, babe. I can walk across the room on my own."

AJ, surprisingly from what I knew about diffidence on the part of former demon minions, didn't back down. "Possession is disorienting for the victim, regardless of its severity. You need to take it easy."

"But I wasn't possessed," Wash protested as he plopped into a chair.

AJ scooted a chair close to Wash and lowered himself into it—not easy with the wings. "You were, love. Just not for very long."

Wash blinked. "Really? I was actually possessed? Did I do anything freaky?"

AJ smoothed Wash's hair back from his forehead and I was hit with another *I-miss-Lachlan* pang. "No. Because I did not allow it."

"You..." Wash's expression softened as he gazed at AJ with total heart-eyes. "Oh, babe. You're amazing." He kissed AJ softly, and probably would have gone a little further if Dr. Mori hadn't cleared her throat.

"Explain, if you please," she said to AJ, although her tone wasn't sharp. More the way Mal or Niall spoke when we were discussing a case: No nonsense, but collegial. Respectful.

"Because of the bond Wash and I share, I felt the possession begin. I..." He swallowed and wiped his forehead—with a third hand. I blinked, because AJ suddenly had at least two extra sets of arms, although they weren't entirely solid, at least to me. "I have enough...experience with possessions myself to recognize the signs." His amiable face hardened in a scowl that rivaled Lachlan's. "I could not allow that to happen to Wash."

"Babe—"

"Mr. Hernandez, *if* you please." She regarded AJ. "Do you know who attempted the possession?"

AJ shook his head. "I was more concerned with Wash. I didn't notice any other demons—I mean, members of the Host —in the vicinity, and we're the only corporeal beings who can possess others."

Corporeal. Uh oh. "Excuse me," I said hesitantly, earning an eyebrow lift from Dr. Mori, "but could a...a *non*corporeal entity possess somebody?"

AJ's eyes widened. "Noncorporeal?"

"Yeah. We've got a situation with some untethered souls on the lam from Sheol."

Dr. Mori frowned. "But surely those entities would be guided to their eventual destinations by the appropriate escort."

I rubbed the back of my neck. How much of this could I disclose? How much did I *want* to disclose? Yannick Tan wasn't technically a client—he'd never signed a contract, even though we'd promised to help him. Hadn't we? Or had I just busted his chops for shirking his duty?

And truthfully? I wanted to help the souls, not him. Him, I just wanted to drop kick into the nearest lava river, along with his specious lawsuit.

"Apparently the only active Ankou has decided to go AWOL," I said. "He told us that he's been overrun with souls since the latest action on the part of the Sheol contract review board."

"So instead of managing his priorities, his solution is to do nothing?"

"Basically, yeah." Although he found time to do one thing: Sue me.

Dr. Mori faced AJ again. "Could one of these untethered souls possess a living being?"

AJ frowned. "I don't really think so? But maybe? Most of the souls in Sheol were humans"—he cut an apologetic glance at me—"who'd contracted for some specific advantage while still in the Upper World. Humans aren't capable of possessing anybody." He spread four of his hands. "Ordinarily, they're the ones being possessed, for whatever benefit the Host's master is trying to reap."

"Don't call them masters," Wash growled.

AJ glanced at Wash fondly. "You may not want to call them masters, love, but when they wield complete control over their Host minions, that is precisely what they are."

"You said *most* of the souls in Sheol are human. But not all, right? Zeke's old supervisor wanted him to score a kangaroo shifter."

"Oh yes," AJ said. "There are supes who made bargains of their own, although ordinarily a supe would work through other channels to achieve what they wished."

I shuddered at that. My friend David had nearly been sacrificed because that jerkface Rodric Luchullain wanted to be royal. Good thing that had backfired.

Dr. Mori tapped irritably on her desk with a Mont Blanc fountain pen. "In other words, we could have an incursion of untethered souls here at United Memorial"—I noted she didn't call it St. Stupid's—"and we have no way of knowing who they are, what they want, nor to what means they'll resort to achieve it."

CHAPTER TWELVE

I cleared my throat. "I might be able to help with at least part of that." I patted my camera bag. "I've got a lens that allows me to see untethered souls. I can't *hear* them, but I could at least check to see if you've got an, er, infestation."

She nodded slowly. "That would be useful, yes. But it won't help us identify the culprit in Mr. Hernandez's attempted possession. Unless"—she locked her gaze on AJ—"you would be able to identify them with the aid of Mr. Mann's enhanced photographic equipment."

"I'm sorry," AJ said. "I couldn't tell by looking. Not whether a particular entity had the intent to possess another, nor who their target might be. However, possessions leave a...a footprint. Were I to evaluate another victim, I could tell if the possessor was the same Host who possessed Wash."

"Possession ballistics," Eleri murmured. "Cool."

I glanced sidelong at Dr. Astell's body. If I pointed my lens at him, would I see his soul hovering around the gurney, or shooting me death—gah! poor choice of words—glares for daring to be human? I wasn't sure I wanted that experience burned into my brain. I mean, it was one thing to run into somebody like Miss Pennybaker, whom I'd never known in life. It was another bucket of herring to stalk an acquaintance in the most private place of all: death.

I raised my hand as though I were back in first grade and needed to visit the boys' room. "If I could ask another question?" When Dr. Mori nodded, I turned to AJ. "I know you do diagnostic possessions to assist with treatment options. Can you do, um, post-mortem possessions? To find out what caused a death?"

AJ blinked at me. "I have never attempted such a thing. Treading the paths of someone's mind when they're living is difficult enough." He hunched forward, wings rustling, wringing at least three pairs of hands. "I have been...within a target before when they...passed."

Wash rested his hand on AJ's nape. "Babe. If this is too painful to remember, you don't have to go there."

AJ's dark eyes, wide behind his bespelled glasses, met Wash's. "No. The past cannot be altered, but perhaps my memories can help us now." He clasped Wash's hand with his fully physical pair. "It was very early in my servitude. I had no experience with passing in and out of a target without hurting them or damaging their memory."

"AJ, I don't mean to add to your stress," I said, "but do you mean that the possession caused the...target's death?"

Wash shot me a narrow-eyed glare, but AJ didn't flinch. "Perhaps. Or perhaps certain other...trauma they had endured at the hands of the mage had caused it instead. There was a...a grace period after the death, however. Not long, but long enough for me to emerge before their soul light was completely extinguished."

"So not all souls linger after death?"

AJ shook his head, raking the fingers of one hand—one of the semi-transparent ones—through his hair, and since his curls moved, I guess his extra arms weren't as incorporeal as they seemed. On the other hand, Miss Pennybaker could type, so who knew what counted as incorporeal anymore?

"If a person is confident in themselves, grounded in their life and choices, I believe they move on immediately."

"Confident in life, confident in death?" Eleri asked.

He nodded. "The souls who resided in Sheol had no choice. As they'd pledged themselves to the demon who contracted with them in life, so they were prevented from moving on to any other plane after death."

That made me feel a little better. I couldn't imagine Dr. Astell, insufferable know-it-all that he'd been, being anything less than confident. "Do you think—"

"Hugh," Eleri muttered, "somebody's trying to get your attention."

I clutched my bag strap, mouth going dry. "Is it Astell?" I whispered—stupid, because Dr. Mori, Wash, and AJ were sitting *right there* and could hear me regardless of how softly I spoke.

"What? No!" She jerked her thumb at the door. "Check it out."

I glanced over my shoulder. The lab's door had a narrow horizontal window set in its upper third, probably just above my eye level. As I watched, a face appeared in the window, then vanished, then appeared again. It's not what you think—it wasn't a supe doing an invisible man routine. It was Ronnie Purl, who was a good six inches shorter than me, jumping up and down so he could see through the glass.

Now that Eleri had called my attention to him, I could hear the faint sound of him calling, "Hugh! Over here!"

I grimaced apologetically at Dr. Mori. "If you don't mind? He's the reason I'm here at all, and I doubt he'll leave until he says his piece."

She cocked an eyebrow. "Ferret shifters are notoriously persistent." She gestured for the door. "Please. But try to be quick."

"I'll do my best." But with Ronnie, who knew? I hurried over to the door and cracked it open. "Ronnie? You doing okay?"

"Me? Oh, sure, sure."

Behind him, Devin rolled his eyes. "Sorry, Hugh. I tried to convince him to talk to you tomorrow, but he insisted."

"No worries. But I don't have much time. What's up?"

Ronnie peered up at me, narrow face intent. "Listen, is it true I came after you with a circular saw?"

"Yeah, but you were mostly unconscious. It was a spasm of some kind."

Rather than apologizing, he scowled. "That's bullshit."

I raised my eyebrows. "Sorry?"

He leaned forward and jabbed a finger at me. "I've been using power tools since I before I could walk—"

"Exaggeration much?" Devin murmured.

"—and I'm telling you, if I'd gone after you with that saw? You'd be half the man you are now. Know what I'm saying?"

I blinked at him. "Are you saying you *intended* to attack me? Or rather Zeke, since he was the one in the saw's path."

That made an impact. He looked absolutely horrified. "Zeke? Ermygerd, I'd *never* do anything to hurt Zeke."

"But I'm fair game?" I said dryly.

He frowned again. "That's not what I mean. It's just..." He sidled closer, glancing right and left as though to make sure nobody could overhear him. "If anybody should ask? Don't mention that I couldn't land that cut, okay?"

I rubbed my forehead. "Let me get this straight. You *want* me to tell people you tried to kill me?"

"What? No! I don't remember anything about that. But if I'd intended to do it, I wouldn't have botched it, okay? I've got my rep to think about."

"Ronnie," Devin said, "maybe give it a rest? Apologize to Hugh for hurting him and then let's go home."

Ronnie turned to his brother. "No, Dev, see, I can't let it stand. Have you ever known me to screw up?"

Devin crossed his arms. "Yes. Frequently."

Ronnie waved the words away. "I mean on a job site. You're the one who taught me. Your cred'll suffer if anyone finds out, too."

"Somehow, I'll survive." Devin smiled at me. "I'm really sorry, Hugh. About your injury." He gave Ronnie an exasperated glare. "And about my clueless brother. Glad you're feeling better. We'll be on our way now."

"Dev, you can't—"

"Hold!" The crack of Dr. Mori's voice froze Ronnie mid-protest. "Bring those men over here immediately."

I met Devin's startled gaze and lifted both hands in surrender. "It's best to do what she says."

"I wouldn't dream of refusing." Devin grabbed Ronnie's elbow when he tried to edge down the hall.

I held the door for the Purls to enter, Dr. Mori gesturing to them peremptorily. As they crossed to her desk, Ronnie caught sight of Dr. Astell's draped body and squeaked.

"Is that a *corpse*?"

"'Fraid so," I said.

"Anybody I know?" he asked out of the corner of his mouth.

I glanced at Dr. Mori, but didn't get a yea or nay from her, no clue about whether I could share the information. So...what the heck. "Actually, it's the ER doctor who treated you today."

Ronnie scoffed. "*That* asshole? He didn't treat me. First thing I saw after I woke up was him backing away from me as fast as he could go. David was the one who fixed me up, him and that other guy, Ewan."

"Mr. Purl," Dr. Mori said, "if you would please stop dawdling and come here." She pointed at the floor in front of her, and I noted that AJ was standing at her shoulder, wringing all eight of his hands this time, while Wash's attempts to pat his back were hampered by his wings. *Yep, total boyfriend reciprocity there.* I wondered briefly whether Lachlan and I would ever be on a level enough playing field to make it possible for us.

Ronnie gulped audibly and shuffled over. "Sorry," he muttered. "Didn't mean to interrupt the autopsy, or whatever."

"My intent is not to chastise you." She gestured to AJ. "With your permission, may AJ lay his hands on you?"

Ronnie gazed at AJ, his eyes wide. "Er…which ones?"

She glanced at AJ. "Will one set suffice?"

AJ nodded, and at Ronnie's shrug, laid his fully corporeal hands on Ronnie's shoulders and closed his eyes. Almost immediately, they flew open again, and he snatched his hands away. "Yes. The same footprint."

"I see." She tapped her chin with one finger—and I was interested to note that her fingernail was definitely a claw. "What is the last thing you remember before you awoke in the ER?"

Ronnie scrunched up his face. "We were at the job site at Quest. I was supposed to frame in the new bathroom walls—because I'm telling you, the one they had in there before was pathetic. I don't know how—"

"Ronnie," Devin said, "keep to the point."

"Oh. Right. Well, like I said, I was supposed to frame in the walls, so I was setting up a couple of sawhorses so I could cut the studs, and then…" He shrugged. "Nothing."

"But you're feeling all right now?"

He glanced from her to AJ. "Sure. Never better." He patted his stomach. "But I could really go for a burger about now."

Dr. Mori favored him with her wintry smile. "Don't let us keep you from your meal. Thank you for speaking with us."

"No problem." He raised a hand to me. "See you around, Hugh."

"Not if we see you first," Eleri murmured as the Purls left, Ronnie's head nearly cranking all the way around in his attempt to keep his gaze locked on Dr. Astell's body.

After Devin closed the door behind the two of them, Dr. Mori gestured for us to be seated again. AJ was only manifesting one additional set of arms, all four hands folded around Wash's, although he'd sprouted an extra set of eyes.

"Since it appears that both Mr. Purl and Mr. Hernandez were possessed by the same entity," she said, her fingers steepled in front of her, "the question remains *how*. Not to mention *who*."

"And why," Eleri said. "Let's not forget that little matter."

"I think I know why," I said, "or at least partly."

Dr. Mori studied me with that *pin-the-specimen-to-the-wall* gaze. "Pray continue."

"Death's taken a holiday."

Her brows lowered. "I beg your pardon?"

"One of the last remaining Ankous—"

"*The* last remaining Ankou," Eleri said.

"—is refusing to escort any of Sheol's recently released untethered souls onward." I spread my hands. "Most of those are human, but some of them could be former demons—members of the Host—right?"

AJ looked thoughtful. "Theoretically, I suppose. Although generally demons don't contract with other demons. If a minion transgressed in any way, their progenitor would simply dismantle their manifestation matrix."

"But it could happen?"

"Yeeesss." He drew out the word, clearly unwilling to go there. "But it would be far more likely that a human soul with sufficient will and enough psychic energy in life could have picked up the way of it over the centuries." He winced. "Some masters weren't appropriately circumspect when it came to hiding their means and methods from those around them, minions and captive souls alike."

"From what Yannick—Slacker Death—said, the recently released souls are clamoring for satisfaction. Now, since he's not around to give it, they're kinda on their own and at large. In fact, one of them has taken up residence in the Quest offices." I hoped Zeke was faring okay with Miss Pennybaker and that none of her untethered buddies had shown up to stake a claim, too. "What if one of them was...well...acting out and sort of"—I waggled one thumb—"hitchhiked a ride on Ronnie?"

"I suppose it's possible," AJ said. "An entity throwing a tantrum?"

"More or less." I glanced at Dr. Astell's still form. "You mentioned that the after-effects of a possession could vary?"

AJ nodded miserably. "If the demon—the Host—possessing the target is skilled, the target may notice nothing at all, except perhaps a loss of time. In other cases, it might not be quite as"—he swallowed—"benign an experience. The target's mind might be completely destroyed." His wings drooped. "Assuming they survive at all."

Eleri leaned forward. "Back in the day, why did you possess anybody, AJ?"

"My masters—"

"*Don't* call them that," Wash growled, earning a smile from AJ—which was probably the point.

"The magicians who controlled my name, then. When one of them wished to acquire something—knowledge, power, riches—they would target the person most likely to provide what they needed."

"So when you"—she made a scooping motion with her hand—"went in, did you, like, know everything they knew? Could other people have figured out that something was off?"

"Early in my captivity, before I had amassed much experience, I wasn't able to do more than wander through the target's mind while they slept. As time went on, I was able to better mimic their actions until I was undetectable." He smiled a little diffidently. "I learned how to make beds when I possessed a chambermaid once, although that wasn't the knowledge that my mast—the mage who controlled me was seeking at the time."

"What happens to *your* body while you're off...wandering?" she asked.

"I can tell you that," Wash said. "It vanishes. He needs an anchor to find his way back, and my heart's in my throat every time in case he gets lost."

AJ turned to Wash and kissed his cheek. "I would not, not with you as my anchor. I will always follow our bond back to you."

"Damn right you will," Wash growled, "or I'll come in and get you."

"Vanishes completely, or simply goes incorporeal?" I gestured to his semi-transparent arms. "Like your extra body parts?"

AJ blinked at me. "I...never thought of it that way, that I'm simply fully in the ether during a possession. But that makes sense, since nothing corporeal could pass through a target without irreparable harm."

I wanted to beg AJ to let me record his possessions with my special lens, just so see whether I could track his progress, but my curiosity would have to wait. "So what you're saying is that you sort of"—I made a pushing motion with both hands—"project yourself into the target and then snap back when you're done, with your anchor to guide you?" AJ nodded. "So what would happen if you didn't have an anchor?"

He blinked, his lips parting in apparent shock. "I...I would have to remain where I was. Within the other forever."

"Or else hop into somebody else?"

"Holy crap," Eleri muttered.

"What if the soul followed Yannick to Quest, got pissed because Yannick was ghosting it, and decided to take matters into its own hands and thumb a ride with Ronnie? Since it didn't have a body of its own or an anchor to keep it, well, anchored, it would have to hang out inside Ronnie for good." I gestured to Wash. "Unless it found a better option and decided to hop the rails."

Eleri elbowed me in the side. "Mixing your travel metaphors much, Hugh?"

"Shut up. I'm trying to make a point," I muttered, then raised my voice back to its normal volume. "Think about it. Ronnie wasn't exactly a prime specimen at the time, concussed and broken-armed as he was. Maybe the soul-hopper—"

"Wouldn't it be more a hopper-soul?" Eleri asked.

I glared at her. "Semantics? Now? Seriously?"

She shrugged. "Clarity is important. Words have consequences, Hugh."

"How about hopper, then? Will that make you happy?"

"It'll do."

I huffed. "Good. Back to Ronnie. Maybe the *hopper* decided to give him up as a bad bet."

Wash shook his head. "Nope. Sorry. That doesn't fly. I didn't show up at the ER until after Ronnie had already been discharged. I'd never been near him." He looked at AJ. "How much range are we talking about?"

"With no corporeal body? Not far. I'm most effective if I'm within touching distance, although I've managed twenty feet or so provided I have a clear line of sight. For an entity with less experience, their control would be marginal at best."

"Could they go incorporeal again?" I asked. "Float around until they could glom onto somebody else?"

AJ frowned in thought for a moment, but then shook his head. "I don't know for certain, but I think it would be very unlikely. The possession itself takes a toll on the demon—the Host—as well. Untethered souls have relatively little energy of their own. Once it took the first hop, it would need the living energy of another target to survive."

"Now we're talking about dead people surviving," Eleri said. "This day just keeps getting weirder."

"If that's the case..." My shoulders tensed, scalp prickling, because I really didn't like this notion. AJ was going to like it even less and Wash might go full on Lachlan Brodie. "...what if our hitchhiker hopped from Ronnie to, well, him?" I pointed at Dr. Astell. "Ronnie said Astell was the first person he saw when he woke up, and when Eleri and I arrived, Renee told us the doctor was hiding in his office, refusing to treat anybody. I'd think someone who had no idea how to successfully integrate themselves into a target"—could we call them a host when the possessor was also a Host? My head was starting to ache—"wouldn't be able to pick up skills as complex as medical procedures." I turned to Wash. "Did you touch Astell?"

Wash rubbed the back of his neck, eyebrows bunched. "I passed him a clipboard. Our hands might have brushed, but I don't really remember."

"Time loss," Eleri murmured.

"Did you notice, AJ?"

He shook his head. "I was discussing a case with the charge nurse. It was only when I felt the possession across our bond that I turned back to Wash. There were quite a number of people around by then because Dr. Astell had collapsed."

"Without confirmation we can't be completely certain," I said, "but my guess is that the hitchhiker hopped from Ronnie, who probably sustained little damage because he was unconscious for most of the event, to Astell, who didn't fare as well, to Wash until AJ booted it out. The question is where"—I glanced from one to another of our morbid little group—"or rather, *who* are they now?"

CHAPTER THIRTEEN

Eleri and I left the medimagical diagnostic team discussing measures for protection against possession and debating whether AJ should try a post-mortem peek at Dr. Astell's, er, footprint.

"We need to find Slacker Death and force him to get back on the job," I growled as we headed for St. Stupid's translocation portal.

"What, so now you're going to counter-sue him?"

"It's a thought."

"Yeah, a terrible one," she said. "You never know who'll be sitting on the tribunal. What if it's somebody with a bias against humans?"

I turned to her in the portal's antechamber. "That doesn't matter if it gets Yannick's ass in gear." If worse came to worst, I might lose my access to the supernatural community. I might lose *Lachlan*. A sharp pain arrowed through me and I rubbed my chest, right under my heart. *Steady, steady. That's not a slam-dunk.* After all, humans were allowed to interact with selkies—or rather, vice versa—and I was now married to him according to their traditions. But that was a side issue. I jabbed my finger in the direction of the diagnostics lab. "Yannick's negligence has *killed* somebody."

She gripped my forearm, a few leafy tendrils—sans thorns, thank goodness—sprouting from her fingertips to wrap around my wrist. "But, Hugh, if the lawsuit goes his way, his advocate could argue that *you're* responsible, since according to the suit, you're the reason the souls are untethered in the first place, regardless of whether Yannick is falling down on the job."

"But I was on a Quest assignment. Won't that be covered by our E&O spells?"

"Maybe. Like I said, if the tribunal's biased, and his advocate is good enough…"

"Crap," I muttered, running my free hand through my hair. I'd faced the tribunal before, and it hadn't been a picnic, even when I'd been innocent—at least of the charges on the table. But weighing that experience against more potential fatalities? I'd take my chances. "Maybe that happens and maybe it doesn't. But the fact is that no matter what caused the problem, Yannick is the only one who can fix it. Finding him has got to be our first step."

"Okay, if that's what you want." She released me and did some hand-wavy thing that made the opaque portal dissolve into a Faerie meadow. "How do you propose we do that?"

We stepped across the threshold. Now, ordinarily, I'd have my usual *Holy crap, this is so cool!* reaction to Faerie, and rubberneck my unhurried way behind my guide. But not today. Today I just wanted to get back to the office by the quickest possible route, so I powered along the path at the foot of Faerie's central tor, next to the river that—according to David— occasionally flooded like a scene from *Lord of the Rings*. He'd told me he'd always wondered whether the director or the production designers had actually been to Faerie. It wasn't the oddest notion.

Heck, *I* was here, wasn't I? And I had first-hand experience of how successfully most supes could pass for human any day of the week.

"Goddess, Hugh, *slow down*."

I glanced behind me to see that Eleri was a good ten feet behind me. She was shorter than me by several inches, although she'd gotten marginally taller since I'd met her. That was a dryad thing, apparently. While humans stopped growing in their teens, dryads kept growing their whole lives, but slowly. You know, like trees. Although apparently their growth could be stunted by certain conditions, such as being a jerk with a shriveled conscience, like her former clan chief.

At the moment, though, Eleri was, well, petite. I heaved a sigh and waited for her to catch up. "Sorry. I just want to *do* something."

"I get it. I do. But you're still not allowed to wander around Faerie on your own, so how about not giving the potential tribunal any more fodder for sanctioning you, okay?"

I grimaced. "Sorry. You're right."

"Of course I'm right," she said, her snub nose in the air. I linked my elbow with hers to keep myself to her pace. Luckily, she was just as anxious to get on with it as I was, so although we weren't exactly sprinting, we weren't dawdling either.

"But so am I. I mean, we're an investigation agency," I said. "Finding people is what we do."

"One of many things." Eleri steered me away from the river toward a copse of birch—she always used trees to transition in and out of Faerie when she had the choice. "Although you'll note that we haven't had much luck with our original mandate —finding the Disappeared."

"True." Quest had been formed when the Faerie rulers had tasked our bosses with finding the Celtic fae who'd vanished over the centuries. I was starting to believe the Disappeared *wanted* to remain hidden, which was their prerogative. "But Yannick is another story. He's been in our office. I'm sure Doop could catch his scent." My steps faltered. "No. Not Doop and definitely not Jordan."

She tilted her head. "Okay, I know why *I* don't want to put them on the trail, but what's your reasoning?"

I knew perfectly well that Jordan was an adult—at least technically. He was over twenty-one, close to twenty-two, and werewolves ordinarily transitioned from junior to senior when they hit twenty-one or thereabouts and finished their Howling. But Jordan's Howling had been interrupted by the werewolf pack re-org, and regardless of his age, he still had a childlike innocence about him that I never wanted him to lose.

"The hopper has killed one person, seriously injured another, and who knows what would have happened to Wash if AJ hadn't booted it out. No way do I want that thing anywhere near Jordan." It didn't matter that Jordan claimed werewolves were tougher than they looked, or that Doop was a literal hellhound.

No. Just no.

"Good." She nodded decisively. "We're on the same page then. He can keep tracking thieves. I'll help him, but I'm here if you need me, Hugh." She squeezed my arm. "That's what BFFs do."

My throat tightened, so I just nodded rather than try to speak as she led us into the trees and then magically out into the Quest fourth floor corridor.

"I don't suppose it's likely Yannick showed up again while we were gone?" she said as we trotted down the stairs. "We don't know why he disappeared in the first place."

"He probably heard a brewski calling."

"Don't be bitter, Hugh. It doesn't become you."

I grunted. "Fine. But he'd already said his piece. Why linger after he'd made his point?" I paused on the staircase, halfway between the second and third floors. "Listen. Do you hear that?"

"Hear what?" She cocked her head. "Oh. It sounds like the world's tiniest hatchet."

"No." I ran down the remaining stairs and through the archway into the Quest lobby. "It's a freaking manual typewriter."

Sure enough, Zeke was once more occupying his own chair and in charge of his keyboard and monitors, but a vintage Underwood No. 5 sat on the desk next to him, in front of a wooden ladder-back chair. A sheet of paper was rolled onto the platen and as we watched, the end-of-line bell dinged and the carriage return lever slapped sideways with a decisive *thwack*.

Zeke was peering at the paper, nodding, not looking up at us. "Yes. I suppose that would work. But—" He caught sight of us, but instead of smiling with his usual welcome, he bit his lip. "Oh. You're back."

"We are." I approached cautiously. "Is that a problem?"

"Not exactly," he said as the typewriter clacked. "But we were hoping to have a few things settled before you returned."

I raised my eyebrows. "'We?'"

"Miss Pennybaker and I." He smiled at the air next to him.

"Zeke?" Eleri moved closer to the desk. "Are those new glasses?"

He touched the frames with one finger. "Yes. Do you like them?"

I frowned. They didn't look that different from his old glasses. "Did you need the vision spell refreshed or something?" It had never occurred to me that the spells that allowed a Sheol-native Host to see in the Upper World might fade over time.

"No. The old spell was doing its job, but these have an upgrade." He smiled at the air again. "I'm able to see Miss Pennybaker now."

I blinked. "Um, cool?"

He nodded. "Absolutely. It's making things so much easier." He glanced sidelong at Miss Pennybaker's location. "Although occasionally more alarming."

"Alarming?" Eleri studied him, her head titled to one side. "How?"

"I get it." I patted my camera bag. "It's not just Miss Pennybaker you can see. You can see other untethered souls, too. It can be a little freaky." Several typebars jammed on the Underwood as though Miss Pennybaker had hit multiple keys at once. "Sorry. I don't mean that *you're* freaky. Only that seeing unseen things can be a little...disorienting."

The Underwood clattered again, and if you don't think a typewriter can sound intimidating? All I can say is you've never met Miss Pennybaker.

Zeke peered at the paper. "She says apology accepted."

Eleri leaned one hip against the desk. "Maybe whoever upgraded your vision spell could figure out a way for Miss Pennybaker to speak. You should ask them."

"I would if I could, but I don't know who it is. The package didn't have a return address, and the postmark was blurred."

My eyebrows rose. "You got special glasses from a secret admirer? Isn't that a little…dangerous? I mean, you don't know where they've been!"

Zeke shrugged. "Since they're doing the job, my only concern is to appropriately thank the sender." He smiled softly. "I think Hamish is responsible. Not for the spell, but for finding somebody who could cast it, a witch or druid."

I could definitely see that. Hamish was incredibly attuned to Zeke's needs. But still… Demons were highly susceptible to influence from unscrupulous mages. I made a mental note to track down the shipment. For now, I returned to the issues at hand. "So, what exactly did you hope to have settled?"

"You have some, um, visitors."

Hope—mixed with a little *it's-about-freaking-time*—warmed my middle. "Did Yannick come back?" Maybe we didn't have to figure out how to track him after all. "Upstairs?" I ran toward the stairs. Zeke called after me, but I didn't want to give Yannick a chance to disappear again. Zeke had put him in the Little Conference Room before, so I headed there first. When I threw open the door, however, it wasn't Yannick in his skater-boy chic who stared back at me.

Nope. It was an entire room full of selkies, including Calum MacGregor with his stupid broom. As soon as they spotted me in the doorway, they all rose, beaming, and bowed. "Your Highness," they murmured in a chorus like waves on the shore.

"Awp!" I ducked back into the hallway, slamming the door closed. Dang it, why didn't these things lock from the outside? I hurried down the corridor and ducked into the next room, a larger conference room, and shut the door, leaning my head against it as I caught my breath. At least I could lock this one.

But as I flicked the lock, someone behind me said, "Ah, Mr. Steinitz." The plummy voice reverberated in the room. "I was wondering when you might grace me with your presence."

I turned slowly. There, silhouetted against the windows, his flaming hair leaping around his *very* sharp-toothed face, was Paimon, Auditor General of Sheol. At least this time he was wearing more than a speedo. "Sir? What brings you here?"

CHAPTER FOURTEEN

Paimon spread his clawed hands. "Why, anticipation, of course. I'm *dying* to see how my photoshoot came out. And please. Call me Paimon. We're friends now, after all."

We were? "Oookaay." In all the chaos since the photoshoot—had it really happened only this morning?—I'd almost forgotten about it. "Well, the thing is, there have been some… complications so I don't have anything ready exactly." Or at all. "However, if you'll wait here for a few minutes, I can print a proof sheet for you so you can select the best shots."

He tutted with his forked tongue. "Nonsense, my boy. You were photographing *me*. Surely *all* the shots are the best."

In a way, he had a point. Paimon was nothing if not *extra*—especially in certain areas I'd prefer not to recall—but he was undeniably photogenic. Maybe it was a Host magic thing. "Still, I'd rather you reviewed them before we make any final decisions."

"Of course, of course. You must forgive an ancient"—he leered—"but still hot Host for his impatience. But since I absolutely cannot wait another instant, I shall accompany you."

I frowned at his wingspan, which was easily six feet wider than AJ's. "I'm not sure you can fit into my office. It's a little small."

He chuckled. "No need to worry about that. I can dance on the head of a pin if I so desire. Lead the way."

I unlocked the door and gestured for him to precede me into the corridor, peeking out before I joined him in case, you know, *selkies*. The LCR door was still closed and none of Lachlan's fan club had ventured into the hallway. Yet. But who knew when they'd kick over the traces? "If you'll come—"

"Hsst! Hugh!" Eleri's voice emanated from beyond the curve in the hall. "Come here. Quick!"

I glanced at Paimon. "I'm, um, not alone, Eleri."

"We're about to be not aloner. Now get over here."

"I don't think *aloner* is a word." I turned to Paimon. "If you'll excuse me?"

"Are you joking? I'm *dying* to know what's going on." He heaved an enormous sigh. "Sheol is so *boring* lately, now that the population density has decreased and our torment quotas have been restricted to almost *nothing*."

So as I walked toward Eleri's voice, Paimon strolled along behind me, heating my backside like a driftwood bonfire.

When the two of us rounded the curve and Eleri spotted my companion, her eyes widened. *"Awp!"*

"That's what I said," I muttered, "but for a different reason. What's up?"

She jerked her thumb at the door of our current staff lounge, the one that the upstairs renovation was supposed to replace. "So many things. Take a look."

I cracked the door and opened it enough that I could stick my head in—then promptly ducked back out as a Frisbee flew at me. "What the— Are Jordan and Doop indulging in a little playtime?"

She shook her head grimly. "Check again."

I crouched down, in case whoever was in there was just waiting to launch a head shot when I reappeared. I eased forward, ready to leap back to avoid any lethal plastic discs. A Frisbee was certainly flying through the air. In fact, *three* Frisbees were in flight. However, none of them appeared to be aimed at me. Instead, it looked like a game of catch—and maybe keep-away—with invisible participants.

Water was running in the sink in the corner, glasses floating under the flow to be filled, only to be dumped out and refilled again. Several of Zeke's vintage teacups were floating across the room, being narrowly missed by the Frisbees.

There was more—soda cans being juggled in the corner, for instance, which I fervently hoped would not be popped open any time soon—but I'd seen enough. I eased the door closed. "We have *got* to find Yannick. Like now."

"I admit it's a little like souls gone wild in there," Eleri said, "but they don't seem to be hurting anything."

"Maybe not yet," I growled, "but who knows when that could change?"

Paimon laid a hand over the Hunter's Moon logo on his T-shirt. "May I?"

Eleri and I shared a look, but from her bland expression, I guessed she didn't know whether getting Paimon involved would be good or bad any more than I did. But then, how exactly did you refuse the Auditor General of hell?

He flung open the door and strode inside, his wings clearing the doorway neatly before snapping open to span the entire width of the room. His hair flames leaped nearly to the ceiling. He crossed his arms, not saying a word. He didn't have to.

Because in the instant it took for the untethered souls to register his presence, everything dropped: the Frisbees, the soda cans, the water glasses, and even poor Zeke's lovely teacups. Everything crashed to the ground, and the room was silent except for the rush of water in the sink. Paimon lifted one flaming eyebrow in that direction and it abruptly shut off.

"If you can scare the crap out of somebody who's already dead," Eleri murmured to me, "we're gonna need a big-ass etheric pooper scooper."

"I'm not looking through my lens to find out, thanks."

Paimon turned to us. "There. Problem solved."

"How, exactly?" I held up both hands. "Yeah, I know you broke up the party—not to mention Zeke's teacups—but is anything actually *solved*? They're still here, right? The souls?"

Paimon flicked one claw and the teacup shards lifted into the air and reformed, like a film running in reverse. Since they floated quickly and jerkily to their shelves, I assumed that they were being transported by the souls.

"Guess that answered one question," I muttered. I cleared my throat and stepped into the room. "Uh, hello. I know you're all a little"—I glanced sidelong at Paimon—"stressed at the moment, but if you'll wait here *quietly*, rest assured that the Quest Investigations staff will do everything we can to resolve your issues satisfactorily."

I turned to Paimon and jerked my head toward the door. He got the message, smirking at me before sauntering into the hallway. Eleri and I followed, and I shut the door behind me.

"Nicely done, Hugh." Eleri patted my arm. "Do you suppose we should send Zeke up with scones so that you're not blowing smoke out your ass?"

I glanced at her sourly. "Can untethered souls even eat? Besides, refreshments don't prove truth or falsehood."

"True, but they make waiting easier to bear." She grinned. "Maybe Miss Pennybaker can serve them. Heck, maybe she can bake them."

"Sophronia Pennybaker?" Paimon grimaced. "Lucifer's balls, if *she's* here, those poor buggers in there will never come out from under the table. She scares *me*."

I shrugged. "Zeke seems to like her." I hiked my camera bag strap up onto my shoulder. "If it's not an impertinent question, do you know what she was doing in Sheol? She doesn't seem the type."

Paimon chuckled. "It's most definitely impertinent, but then, I appreciate impertinence. She was a follower of the Pankhursts in the UK and contracted for women's suffrage, of course. Votes for women." His grin turned evil. "However, while she intended the contract to be for *all* women everywhere, she left the terms vague enough that the demon who made the deal limited his side of the bargain. UK only, women over thirty, plus a lot of other requirements about education and property ownership. She's been pissed off ever since."

"Can't blame her for that," Eleri said. "Especially since full suffrage *still* hasn't happened."

I peered up at Paimon. I'd gotten by with one question. Could I risk another? "Now that all these souls are on the loose, do you know how we can corral them and get them to move on?"

He shrugged. "Get a psychopomp."

"Yeah, that's a problem. The only one we know is MIA at the moment." I turned to Eleri. "Maybe we should contact Herne to track him down. I mean, given that Yannick's not meeting his responsibilities, could that be construed as oath-breaking?"

Eleri screwed up one side of her mouth. "That's kind of a gray area, Hugh."

"It's worth a shot, though, right?"

"If I may make a recommendation?" Paimon said with surprising diffidence. "If you bring the Hunter into this, you might want to keep him separate from the souls herein. Some of those relegated to Sheol were sent there by Herne himself when they tried to renege on their bargains. They might take his presence amiss."

"Like they took yours?" I asked dryly.

He shrugged. "They can do nothing to me, nor to Herne— although many of them rejoiced at his brief incarceration. But an angry soul can wreak havoc when it's abroad with no constraints." He shrugged again. "Poltergeists get the much of the blame for that, but they're not always the ones heaving hardware about."

Zeke had warned about much the same thing, and we'd already had evidence of at least one vengeful soul. The question was—

"Ow!" I clapped a hand to my shoulder. "What the—"

"Speak of the devil," Paimon murmured.

Another invisible blow landed on my arm. "Whoever you are, you've got my attention. Please stop hitting me." I held up my hands. "Taking out my camera now so I can see you, all right?" I waited a moment to make sure no further blows were forthcoming, then unzipped my bag and slowly withdrew my camera. The telephoto lens was still mounted on it from before. When I peeked through the viewfinder, I was unsurprised to see Miss Pennybaker, although I hadn't expected her to be brandishing a furled umbrella like a battle axe.

"Um, is there something I can do for you, ma'am?" I winced. Without her typewriter, how would she let me know?

"She says there's somebody downstairs," Paimon drawled, polishing his claws on his shirt.

"Sure. Zeke."

He shook his head. "Nope. He's been sent out in search of sushi by your other guests."

Eleri's eyebrows shot up. "Untethered souls can eat sushi? Guess we don't need ethereal scones after all."

"Not those guests." Paimon jerked his thumb at the staff room door and then pointed back down the hallway. "The other ones."

Eleri's eyebrows rose. "We have other guests? Anybody cool?"

"Don't ask," I muttered, "but if a white-haired guy comes after you with a broom, run, because he's not here to tidy up." I peered in Miss Pennybaker's general direction. "Is it Jordan? Werewolf? Early twenties? Brown hair and eyes?"

"That's a negative as well," Paimon said.

Eleri patted my arm. "Don't worry, Hugh. I'll take care of it until Zeke gets back. You"—she glanced up at Paimon—"take care of business up here."

She turned to go, heading straight for Miss Pennybaker, so I caught her arm and steered her toward the wall. She frowned at me, confused. I shrugged. "Avoiding collisions is only polite."

Her expression cleared. "Ah. Got it." She beckoned. "This way, ma'am." She trotted around the curve in the hallway, and I watched through the lens as Miss Pennybaker tucked her umbrella under her arm and followed.

"Interesting woman," Paimon mused.

"Miss Pennybaker?"

"No. The dryad. Do you suppose she'd go out with me?"

I gave him *get-real-dude* look. "Seriously? For one thing, you're on fire."

He grinned toothily. "Yes, I am *tres* hot."

"That's not what I mean." I pointed to his hair. "You're *literally* on fire. Dryads aren't okay with open flames. Besides..." Despite my best efforts, my glance cut down toward his groin. "You've got the wrong equipment. In more ways than one."

He heaved a sigh. "It was worth a try."

"Come on. I'll get you that proof sheet. Once you decide which shots you want, I'll get them printed up for you."

"Excellent. I'll need *many* copies. Money is no object."

"I'd prefer payment in untethered soul remediation," I said sourly as we headed to my office.

"Not my job," he said cheerfully.

"Yeah." I sighed. "That's what they all say."

CHAPTER FIFTEEN

After Paimon left with his proof sheet—although he'd spent at least fifteen minutes with my loupe, *ooh*ing and *aah*ing over the frames—I pulled out my phone to text Herne. Before I hit *send*, though, I glanced around my cramped office. If Herne was sporting his antlers at the moment, it would be a tight fit. Yes, he'd gotten a special spell that allowed him to pass through any doorway, but he still needed elbow room—so to speak—once he passed the threshold.

If this were an ordinary day, I'd take him to one of the conference rooms or the staff lounge, but considering what I'd encountered up there already? I'd prefer to stay far, far away. Who knew what else might be lurking behind closed doors?

However, this would hopefully be a quick conversation, one that didn't require scone-based negotiations. So I headed up to the fourth floor translocation portal. If Herne was feeling peckish, I could always grab a soda and a bag of chips for him out of the vending machines. If he was in a more businesslike mood, we could just have our chat in the hallway and he could be off. Although... The corridor didn't have a window. Had night fallen? Herne traveled *on the night*, so he'd need darkness to track down Yannick. Jeez, this day was shaping up to be the longest in my life, maybe in all of history.

My belly swooped and shimmied. *I've been married for almost a whole day.* Yet somehow I'd managed to put it out of my mind.

Granted, that particular complication had been overtaken by events, so to speak, but I'd imagined my wedding day—and wedding night—to be very different.

Before I could open that whole Pandora's box of feelings, though, I had more pressing concerns—an AWOL Ankou and a rampaging hopper-soul. I'd best get those two handled. My own personal drama could wait.

I hurried up the stairs to the fourth floor, my camera held in front of me like a shield. Thankfully, I didn't spot any untethered souls meandering the hallways as I hustled past the vending machines to the portal. I keyed in the code for Faerie, but I didn't open the door. Not yet. Instead, I pulled up the text app on my phone.

Me: Hey, Herne. We've got a situation here. We could really use your help.

The ellipsis danced on the screen. Disappeared. Popped up again.

HtHunter: I am somewhat engaged at the moment.

I grimaced. Not good.

Me: If you're out chasing prey, I get it. But this is kind of an emergency.

HtHunter: As it happens, I have an assignation.

Okay, translating…

Me: Do you mean you have a date? Eleri would be thrilled, considering she'd been wanting to set Herne up since that homicidal angel Athaniel had catfished him. *Is it with Wyn?*

More ellipsis hide and seek. Then finally—

HtHunter: I will be there presently.

Me: Great! I'm waiting at the Quest Faerie portal.

I opened the door, expecting to have to hang out for a while, but Herne was already there, ankle deep in the lush meadow grass with a bouquet of purple and yellow wildflowers in his hands. Instead of his usual vaguely medieval garb, he was wearing a fitted gray button-down with the sheen of silk and black dress trousers. He sported a full rack of antlers, but no attendant hellhounds.

I blinked. "Wow. You look really nice."

His brown cheeks flushed rosy. "Do you think so? I don't wish to embarrass my...date."

"Trust me. You won't. Although..." I jerked my chin at the antlers. "Those might get in the way in most traditional date venues."

He flushed darker. "I am aware. However, Wyn is...pleased by my antlers, so I wanted to meet him with them in place. I shall shed them before our dinner, however."

I rubbed the back of my neck. "Yeah, about that. I hate to interrupt date night, but I was hoping you could track down somebody for us."

He frowned. "You are aware I can only track those I know or those who are my rightful prey."

"Yes, I know. But I think this guy might qualify as prey. He's not doing his job, and as a result, we've already had two injuries and one confirmed death. We want to locate this guy and get him back in the harness before things get any worse."

Herne nodded thoughtfully. "He may indeed qualify. What is his name and the charge he has failed to meet?"

"His name's Yannick Tan, and he's—"

"An Ankou." I couldn't read his expression. Regret? "I am not certain I can help you. I know of Yannick, although we have never met face to face."

"I doubt you'll be impressed when you do."

"I'm not certain I can pursue him as I ordinarily would. He and I are...in the same line of work, albeit our tasks fall at different times. I dispatch miscreants' mortal shells, after which time Yannick or one of his cohorts escorts their soul onward."

"In other words, you handle different parts of the deathly supply chain?" I asked dryly.

"As you say." Herne shrugged one shoulder. "Consequently, it may constitute a...a..."

"Conflict of interest?"

"Aye. A conflict, for me to pursue as prey a person who is ordinarily a colleague."

"Well, this particular colleague is causing problems. He's refusing to escort souls onward."

Herne's eyebrows bunched. "Why?"

"Because there are too many of them."

The divot between his brows deepened. "That makes no sense. There will never be any fewer unless he escorts them one by one."

"Exactly my point. But he's not buying it. He's taken a powder—"

"Powder?" His eyebrows reversed course. "He is stealing cosmetics?"

"Sorry. I mean, he's vanished, and one of the souls he's left behind has turned homicidal." If Herne had an issue tracking Yannick himself, maybe we could work around that. "I don't suppose you could track down the homicidal soul, could you?"

He shook his head. "Nay. My purview is the living. My mission ends when they no longer walk the mortal plane."

Crap. Well, it had been worth a try. "Do you think you could track down Yannick for us, though? Before any other innocent people suffer?"

Herne's expression darkened. As imposing as he was, and as freaked out as any guilty party got in his presence, he was *really* passionate about seeing justice done. "I will do my best, although I cannot promise success."

"That's all I can ask. Thanks, man." I gestured at the flowers. "And sorry for interrupting date night."

Herne's smile softened briefly. "He will understand. He neither fears nor resents my calling." There was that blush again. "He finds it…arousing. So when I return—"

"Yep. Okay. That's good." Really didn't need to know what Herne and Wyn got up to, especially when Lachlan and I had yet to get up to anything other than polar bear impressions.

"Thanks again." I raised one hand in farewell and shut the door. "Whew!"

I wondered whether Zeke had gotten back with the selkies' snacks. Could he have ordered from a Portland restaurant, or would he have had to go farther afield, maybe through Faerie? I keyed open the door and peered out across the Faerie landscape. I didn't see anything moving nearby, so if Zeke *was* using Faerie as a food delivery shortcut, he hadn't made it back yet.

I shut the door and scuttled down the stairs, keeping an eye out through the camera lens for any invisible interlopers. But the coast remained clear all the way into the lobby.

In fact...

"Didn't Miss Pennybaker say somebody was waiting here?" I scanned the room, including under the chairs because you never knew. But other than Eleri in Zeke's chair and Miss Pennybaker sitting straight-backed behind the Underwood, the place was empty.

Eleri shrugged. "No, *Paimon* said somebody was here." The Underwood's keys clattered, and the carriage returned smartly. Eleri checked the paper. "Miss Pennybaker says Paimon takes liberties with the text. Actually, it was a phone call." Eleri's brow wrinkled in thought. "We need to figure out a way to synthesize her voice so she can answer the phone."

"Uh..." I tucked my camera back in the bag. "I don't mean to be rude, but why?"

Eleri rolled her eyes. "Really, Hugh, it should be obvious. So she can cover the office, of course. You can't expect her to hunt one of us down every time the phone rings. It's a perfectly reasonable accommodation."

"But—" I sighed, because I really didn't want to bring up the fact that once we found Yannick, it was entirely possible that Miss Pennybaker would be moving on and unavailable for continued employment at Quest or anywhere else. I decided to defer that conversation until it was actually necessary. "So, who was on the phone?"

Eleri shifted from contemplative to businesslike. "Dr. Mori. She said that the staff has tracked down all the patients who were in the ER between when Ronnie was admitted and when Dr. Astell collapsed." She grimaced. "There were a lot of them. We've got a list." A piece of paper rose from the desk and floated toward Eleri. She took it with a smile at—presumably—Miss Pennybaker, who, it seemed, could take dictation too. "Most of them were fine, but at least one of them had the same possession footprint, so they're tracking down all of his contacts."

I frowned. "But won't the trackers be in danger of possession too, if the hopper decides to take another body for a spin?"

She shook her head. "AJ and Dr. Mori came up with a combination of herbs that should ward off possession, and the witches in the St. Stupid's pharmacy ran with it. They filled up enough little charm bags to protect the staff. Wash and AJ are handling the outreach to the patient, and since AJ can deflect anybody who dares to possess Wash, they're in no danger. Dr. MacLeod has his students hard at work manufacturing more anti-possession charms, too, so anybody who's likely to come in contact with the hopper will have protection."

"Yeah, but how do we know who'll come in contact with it? We don't know where it is. It could be anywhere in Portland, for all we know." For that matter, if the hopper had glommed onto somebody who'd taken the FTA home, they could be anywhere, *including* Faerie. If the hopper were to possess the King or Queen? I shivered. Nope. Not happening. We'd find Yannick, corral the renegade soul, and force Slacker Death to get it the hell out of Dodge.

CHAPTER
SIXTEEN

"Hugh?" Eleri leaned her elbows on the desk, a frown pleating her forehead. "You're looking uncharacteristically warlike. Weren't you able to contact Herne?"

"I reached him, yes. But he may or may not be able to help us."

"Why not?"

"He and Yannick are on a kind of"—I sketched a circle in the air—"death-trajectory relay team, a weird connection that complicates things. Herne's not okay with innocents suffering, though, so he said he'll do his best." I winced. "Although he wasn't thrilled that I interrupted his date night."

Eleri perked up at that. "Date night? Who with? It's Wyn, isn't it?" She leaned toward Miss Pennybaker's chair and whispered, "Didn't I tell you?" The Underwood clacked in response and Eleri nodded. "Oh, yeah. Total hotties, both of them."

"Wait a minute." I glanced between my alleged BFF and the spot in the air where she'd aimed her grin. "Are you *gossiping* with Miss Pennybaker?"

Eleri sniffed. "She's a very good listener. And it's not gossiping when it's case review."

"Case review. Right."

"Oh, come on, Hugh, don't be a stick in the mud. Admit it. There was a definitely spark there."

"Yeah, he seemed pretty, er, sparky. So hopefully he'll be able to nab Yannick and get back to his date." Nobody knew better than I did how off-putting constant interruptions could be to a relationship's development. Although the latest interruption to my own relationship had been...well...marriage.

"Pardon me?"

I turned at the soft, vaguely familiar voice. Tholo Innes, the changeling who'd assisted in our last case, stood in the archway, accompanied by a kid no more than ten or so. The kid uttered a squeal of excitement and rushed past me to plant both hands on the desk and beam at Eleri.

"Hi! You're Eleri. I can tell because dryads always smell like trees after the rain and turkey stuffing."

I buried my laugh at Eleri's affronted expression. Jordan had once compared dryad scent to wet bark, autumn leaves, and sage. This kid was clearly filtering those scents through his own experience.

"Noah." Tholo's tone held gentle patience. "Remember, we don't mention people's smells in public."

Noah blinked up at Tholo with big brown eyes, his hair flopping over his forehead in a very familiar way. "Sorry, Tholo. I forgot."

"Do you remember how to introduce yourself to new people?"

Noah brightened. "Yes!" He turned to Eleri. "How do you do? I'm Noah Tate and I use he/him pronouns."

Eleri's lips twitched, any perceived insult obviously forgiven and forgotten. "How do you do, Noah? I'm Eleri Deilen and I use she/her pronouns." She leaned forward and lowered her voice to a conspiratorial whisper. "Unless I've very much mistaken, you must be related to Jordan Tate."

"How did you guess?" Noah beamed, his smile so familiar that I couldn't stop *this* laugh. Talk about family resemblance. "Oh, it's the name, right? Because we're both Tates." He screwed up his face. "Although lots of people are named Tate. It's not that unusable a name."

"Unusual, Noah," Tholo murmured.

"Right. Unusable. That's what I said." He spotted me. "Oh! Oh! And you're Hugh!"

"Noah," Tholo said.

The mild reprimand didn't dampen Noah's enthusiasm. "How do you do? I'm Noah Tate and I use he/him pronouns."

"You're right, I'm Hugh. He/him." I held out my hand. "I'm pleased to meet you, Noah. We're very fond of your brother here. He's a real asset to Quest Investigations."

Noah glanced from my hand to Tholo. "Is it okay to shake? You know…because?"

"Probably not at the moment." Tholo cast me an apologetic glance. "We appreciate the gesture, Hugh, and any other time it would be fine, but Noah's in a somewhat vulnerable state right now, and we're trying to avoid contact with anybody other than his family members."

I glanced at Noah, who was scratching vigorously behind one ear. "Is he ill?"

"No. But I think he's about to experience his first shift. Young werewolves are quite sensitive to contact during this period and prone to developing strong attachments. It's when their pack bonds begin to solidify."

The Underwood clattered, causing Noah to leap back at first, but then creep forward again, his nose quivering.

Eleri leaned over to check the message and shot a sidelong glance at Tholo before straightening up. "Please know that these are not my words, Tholo, okay?" She cleared her throat. "I quote, 'If that is the case, then what are this child's parents thinking?' Close quote."

Tholo checked on Noah, who apparently hadn't registered Miss Pennybaker's secondhand reprimand. He was on his hands and knees, peering under the desk. "There's nobody hiding under here. How did that typewriter go? And why is there an old typewriter here when you've got a computer, anyway?" He popped his head up to grin at Eleri. "Your boots are really cool!"

"Thank you," she said solemnly. "I like them."

Tholo gazed down at Noah with obvious fondness. "Noah's situation is somewhat unusual. While most of the students at our school are day pupils, we do have some boarders, Noah among them."

"That seems odd," I said. "Aren't werewolf packs extremely close knit? I'd think they'd want to keep him nearby, especially at this point."

"You'd think." Tholo's voice was so completely devoid of inflection that I glanced at him sharply. *He doesn't approve.* But of what? Or whom?

I was about to dig deeper—hey, investigator, right? It's my job to be nosy—when the street door opened, followed by a very familiar clatter of claws on the marble entryway tiles.

Noah scrambled to his feet. "Doop!" He raced for the archway, but Tholo held up a hand.

"Remember, Noah. Think before you act."

"But, Tholo." Wow, talk about puppy-dog eyes. "It's *Doop*."

"Then you will be able to greet him when he arrives."

"All right," Noah said resignedly, although he continued to shift from foot to foot.

I eyed him uneasily. "Is he just excited, or does he need the restroom?"

Tholo's remarkable sea-green eyes crinkled behind his glasses as he chuckled. "I suspect a bit of both."

Judging by the sharp yip, followed by a dismayed shout and the *tha-wump-tha-wump* of paws on the stairs, Doop was just as eager to see Noah as Noah was to see him.

As soon as he appeared in the archway, Noah flung himself at him, wrapping his arms around Doop's neck. I'd never have believed a hellhound could look doting and indulgent, but Doop had it nailed. He let Noah pull him down onto the floor and sprawl over him as though Doop were an extremely furry chaise longue—and incidentally, blocking the entrance completely.

"Oh. I get it now." The person who edged past Doop into the lobby wasn't Jordan—it was Hector Gonzales, another werewolf from the Dog House, the quasi-frat house where Jordan lived with several of his friends. Yeah, frat house werewolves. Go figure. "No wonder Doop made a break for it." Hector shrugged off the Dooper bag and set it on a chair. "Hey, Noah."

Noah beamed up at Hector from atop Doop. "Hi, Hector! Tholo thinks I'm about to shift!"

"Really, dude?" I didn't miss Hector's furtive glance at Tholo, which belied his upbeat tone. "That's awesome!"

"Yeah," Noah said, scratching behind his ear again. "Except it *itches*."

Tholo beckoned Hector and me to follow him to the desk, leaving Noah in the doorway to commune with Doop. "Hector," he murmured, "do you know how to contact Noah's parents? Or the Jackson pack alpha? I'm afraid the shift is imminent and I haven't been able to locate any of them."

Hector rubbed the back of his neck. "Yeah, that might be tough. Jordan and Noah's folks, they've always been what you'd call free spirits."

Somehow, considering Jordan's rather loose interpretation of most rules, I wasn't surprised. "Werewolf hippies?"

"I guess? Anyway, after what happened with Hrodgar's Syndrome, they decided life was too short not to"—he gestured expansively—"revel in the experience. They took off on a wilderness camping trip."

"Which wilderness?" Eleri asked.

Exasperation flickered across Hector's amiable round face. "All of them. They've been gone for months."

"But Hrodgar's Syndrome is history, right?" I glanced from Eleri to Tholo. "Everyone's been inoculated."

"Not quite," Tholo said. "Everyone who could be reached has been inoculated, but not everyone could be reached."

I winced. The Disappeared. Right. Hrodgar's Syndrome was a truly sadistic curse that had been aimed at werewolves, but had been so bungled that it affected the *calons* of all supes, regardless of their species. It had gotten entangled in the magic grid, so it didn't matter where they were—they'd be affected, their own magical nature subverted and twisted until it killed them.

Hector patted my arm. "Don't worry, Hugh. The work-around is still in place."

Ah, the work-around. "You mean Tanner Araya is still the de facto—"

"Supreme alpha of every supe in the universe?" Hector grinned. "Yep. Not that he wants the job. He'd much rather focus on his college classes and his work on supe history with Dr. MacLeod. As soon as the alphas recovered, their packs reaffirmed their loyalty to their original leaders, and Tanner was off the hook. But Jordan's folks"—another of those expansive gestures—"never declared allegiance to the Jackson alpha."

From the rapid *rat-a-tat* from the Underwood, Miss Pennybaker clearly had an opinion. Eleri checked the paper on the platen. "She wants to know why not." She glanced at Noah, who was humming some kind of tune and scratching behind Doop's ears for a change. "I'd prefer not to pass along her more colorful description of people who shirk their responsibilities. For, you know"—she jerked her chin at Noah—"reasons."

"Um..." Hector pointed at the typewriter from behind his other palm, much like Eleri had done, his eyebrows lifted toward his wavy black hair.

"Oh. Sorry." I gestured to the chair. "Hector, Tholo, Noah, may I introduce you to Miss Pennybaker?" I jerked my thumb at the reclining hellhound. "She's already met Doop."

Noah broke off his hum and looked up at me. "If she's a Miss, does she use she/her pronouns?"

"We've been assuming so, but it's probably better to ask," I said with a smile. "She's sitting right there."

Noah's eyes widened. "You mean she's *invisible*? That is *so cool!*" He hurried over to lean against the desk near the Underwood and watched with wide eyes when the keys tapped out a response. "She/her is right, and she thanks us for asking. Most people...reefer?"

"I expect that's *refer*, Noah," Tholo said.

"Most people reefer to one of her kind as *it*." Noah frowned ferociously. "That's just rude. Like people calling Doop a"—he leaned in, lowering his voice to a stage whisper—"a *you-know-what* in a mean way." As though he were afraid Doop might have picked up on the conversation, Noah hurried over to kneel next to him and circle his neck with both arms again.

When Miss Pennybaker attacked the keys once more, I was close enough to see what she'd typed: *How could any respectable werewolf abandon pack and family, neglecting their duties so egregiously?*

I moved aside so Hector and Tholo could see the message. Hector sighed. "Like I said, free spirits. They discovered it suited them much better to have an alpha who...who..."

"Wasn't all up in their business?" Eleri asked.

Hector nodded. "Yeah. I mean, even though they're technically part of Tanner's pack, they don't impose on him. Much. Although all their mail gets delivered to the Dog House." He rolled his eyes. "And they get *a lot* of catalogues."

The Underwood clattered and dinged, and the paper zipped out of the platen. Eleri snatched it out of the air before it reached Tholo. "You don't want to know what she said about *that*." She crumpled the paper and tossed it into the recycling bin as Miss Pennybaker briskly rolled a fresh sheet into the typewriter.

I scratched the back of my head. "Does that mean that Noah is part of Tanner's pack, too?"

"Yes and no," Tholo said. "Noah's still a minor, which in werewolf society has nothing to do with age. Young werewolves can't declare pack allegiance until their first shift. Until that time, their membership defaults to their parents' pack."

"So if we can't locate the Tates, then Tanner has to babysit Noah's shift?"

"I'm not a baby! I'm nine," Noah protested.

"No insult intended, dude," I said.

"Nah," Hector said. "Jordan can step in, since he's a blood relation. We're meeting him here."

My shoulders relaxed a fraction. "You've heard from him then?"

"Sure." Hector patted his jacket pocket. "Texted with him a little while ago."

Eleri narrowed her eyes. "How come you can raise Jordan on his cell, but we can't?"

Hector's dark eyes widened until the whites showed around his irises. "Um…"

"Let me guess," I said. "You've been tweaking the magic grid again with one of your apps?"

He winced. "Maybe?" Hector was that odd supe who was fascinated with human technology. He'd aced all the human computer classes he'd taken. But although he was a gifted programmer, just learning about it wasn't enough for him—he took things to the next level, integrating tech with magic, which wasn't exactly…approved.

"Does Dr. MacLeod know?" Bryce was the unofficial academic mentor for all the Dog House guys.

"Not yet. I'll tell him, I promise, but the app's not out of beta yet. The tracking component is still a little wonky, and I don't want to present it to him until I've worked out all the bugs."

"What did Jordan say in his text?"

"Oh. Just that he was on the trail."

I shared a glance with Eleri. "Following up on that theft?"

She nodded. "He was determined not to let the H&R get in the way."

"Once he gets here," Hector said, "I figured we'd pick up pizza on the way back to the Dog House. Noah can hang out with us there."

"Yay! Pizza!" Noah crowed, and Doop woofed. Noah wrinkled his nose. "No pineapple though, right?"

"Dude!" Hector planted a hand on his chest. "You wound me. Would I ever? Pineapple on pizza is—"

"Just wrong," they said together. I chuckled. Clearly, Noah had already spent time with his brother's friends.

When the kid leaped up, indulging in some wild gyrations around the office as he chanted about pizza toppings, I turned to Tholo. "Do they always get this way before their first shift?"

Tholo smiled wryly. "No. This is pretty much Noah's default state."

"Um, Hugh?" Eleri pointed at my ankle, where Doop was sniffing in a disconcerting manner, his leg twitching ominously.

"Doop!" I said sternly. "You know better. No leg-lifting on friends." The dog sighed heavily but laid down, the cant of his eyebrow tufts telegraphing his reluctance. "Good boy."

"Wow," Hector said. "I'm impressed. Usually he doesn't obey anybody but Jordan that quickly."

"We've got an understanding. Doop's practically a Quest employee."

"Hugh," Eleri said, "I didn't want to say anything, but I don't think Doop was entirely to blame." Her gesture took in my whole body. "You're...a little ripe."

Noah stopped his pizza dance next to Eleri's chair and whispered audibly to her, "I didn't want to say anything, either."

I winced. I was still wearing the scrub shirt I'd cadged from the hospital, and other than the nurses cleaning my wound, I hadn't washed since my plunge in the Pacific. "I'll just head home and take a shower, then, shall I?"

She cocked an eyebrow. "Everyone within ten feet of you would be very grateful. I'm sure Zeke will be back shortly, and in the meantime, Miss Pennybaker and I will hold down the fort."

"Text me with any news?"

She flicked her fingers at me and turned to the computer monitor. "I'll pretend you didn't ask that. Now go."

I went.

CHAPTER SEVENTEEN

No shower had *ever* felt this good. They say that you don't really have sense memory for hot and cold, but try telling my skin that. I was certain it was still in denial about that ocean dip —heck, was it only this morning?—and was sending messages directly to the pleasure centers of my brain: *This is what water is supposed to feel like.*

Humming as I washed my hair, I gave thanks to whoever had built my little rental cottage, because they'd installed an extremely efficient and generous water heater. Yeah, the pipes complained now and then, knocking and groaning, but I didn't care as long as the hot water kept flowing.

For a couple of minutes after I'd rinsed off the last of the soap and shampoo, I stood under the spray, steam billowing around me, and let the warmth seep into my bones. Then I sighed. Unless Zeke, Mal, or Niall had returned, Eleri and Miss Pennybaker were on their own at Quest, if you didn't count the selkies and untethered souls kicking back upstairs. With the hopper still at large, I didn't want to leave Eleri without corporeal backup for too long, so I turned off the water.

But the knocking continued. Not the pipes. Somebody was at my door.

"Crap," I muttered as I reached for my towel. "Who the heck could it be at this time of evening?" Then I froze. *Lachlan.* I hadn't checked in with him. Hadn't told him about the selkie incursion at Quest. Hadn't told him about the possession.

In fact, I was an even worse husband—however inadvertently acquired—to him than Wyn had been. He'd known that Wyn was going into hiding, had even abetted Wyn's flight. But I'd just ghosted him. On our wedding day, no less.

Yeah, Yannick wasn't the only dude in denial about his life.

The knocking stopped as I finished drying myself. I hurried out of the bathroom and through the kitchen to the front door. Now, despite what you might think of me, I'm not *totally* reckless. I didn't throw it open naked without checking. Nope. I wrapped the towel around my waist and peered through the peephole like a responsible adult with a reasonable sense of self-preservation.

Nobody was there.

I sighed, not sure if I was disappointed or relieved. If it had been Lachlan, he'd either return—he was nothing if not stubborn, although he'd probably call it persistent—or I could catch up with him later. Hey, I would totally catch up with him. Eventually. And if it hadn't been Lachlan? If it was the Avon representative or the UPS driver or Jehovah's Witnesses? I had no obligation to follow up. Although, for the UPS driver, I'd at least make an effort.

I trudged into the bedroom and dug out a clean pair of jeans, a thermal henley, *and* a flannel shirt. I'm telling you, no matter what anyone tries to tell you, cold sense memory is definitely a thing. I was pulling on a pair of my warmest socks when the knocking came again.

I stalked toward the door, my stockinged feet sliding a little on the hardwood floor. This time, when I checked the peephole, Lachlan's hopeful face, distorted by the fisheye lens, was peering back at me. I took a deep breath and opened the door.

"Hey," I said.

"Matthew." The way he said my name always sent a frisson down my spine, but this time, his tone was laced with such uncertainty that my belly did a nosedive onto the threshold.

He's not sure of his welcome. And really, could I blame him for that? I hadn't been exactly husband material all day. Heck, I'd barely been slight-acquaintance material.

So I hugged him, right there on my front doorstep. Because he should *never* doubt that I wanted him.

He exhaled in a rush, and I realized he'd been holding his breath, afraid I'd reject him. I hugged him tighter and his arms came around me. As big as he was, I was practically wearing him. *This must be what it feels like for Wash or Quentin when their partners fold them in their wings.*

But you know what? Standing there on my porch, Lachlan's heart beating strong and steady under my cheek, I wasn't envious of those guys at all anymore. Because that closeness, that connection, was right here, mine for the taking.

As long as I wasn't stupid enough to throw it away. And that…remained to be seen.

I tipped my head up. "Want to come in for a minute?"

Darkness had fallen, but his smile glimmered in the wan glow of my porch light. "Only a minute?"

"I need to get back to the office soon, but…we need to talk."

He sighed. "Aye. That we do."

I stood aside to let him walk in and then closed the door. He hesitated in the middle of the living room, probably not sure where he was allowed to go. We'd never made it to my bedroom in the time since his sundering from Wyn. Heck, we'd never even made it to the kitchen again. In fact, I could count the times he'd been in my house on one hand, and how ludicrous was that?

I gestured to my second-hand sofa, its brown corduroy upholstery a little worn on the armrests. "Have a seat?"

He hesitated for a moment, and then sighed and sat at one end, his elbows on his knees, head bowed. *Leaving the choice up to me.*

You know what? Screw distance. After the day I'd had, I needed to be close. I suspected Lachlan needed it just as much. So I sat on the center cushion, near enough to feel his warmth along my side, but not pressed up against him either.

He had a right to choose as well.

"I was afraid you wouldn't let me in."

"Well, I was in the shower the first time you knocked, so I didn't get to the door before you left."

Lachlan frowned. "I didn't leave."

"You didn't knock before? About ten minutes ago?"

"Nay." His expression cleared. "I'll wager it was your young werewolf. I saw him in the woods after the FTA driver dropped me by that cave of yours."

"It's not my cave." I waited for the wave of longing that used to hit me whenever I thought about Ted's cave. But it didn't arrive. *Guess I really have moved on.* "It's...a friend's." And for maybe the first time, I could call Ted a friend without any awkward subtext or regret. "What did Jordan say?"

"We didn't speak. I waved at him as he scampered off into the trees." Lachlan chuckled. "He's a fey one, that laddie, scampering about the woods bare-arsed."

I chuckled. "If he was naked, no wonder he didn't stop to chat. That probably means he'd shifted. He's been tracking some thieves, and he can follow scents better as his wolf." I glanced at the door, biting my lip. "I hope he remembers where he left his clothes." I had a sudden mental image of a naked Jordan standing on my porch, much to the consternation—or maybe avid interest—of my neighbors. "Do you suppose that's why he was here?"

"We don't know it was him. I only saw him in the woods." He nudged my shoulder with his own. "If he needs you, he'll be back."

"I suppose you're right." However, I made a mental note to have Hector use his unauthorized app to tell Jordan the theft case could wait. We had more critical issues afoot.

Lachlan took my right hand in his left, and I noticed a wide gold band on his ring finger. He hadn't worn a ring with Wyn. The sight sent an unexpected jolt through me. Not fear. Not anger. Excitement and...*arousal*? I touched the band with a tentative finger. "Lachlan? What's this?"

His shoulders rose and fell as his grip tightened on my hand. "Whatever you feel about jumping the besom with me, Matthew, whether you choose never to accept me as your mate or not, in my heart, you're my husband now. I know I have no right to claim you, but—"

I laid my finger over his lips. "Lachlan. It's not that I don't see a future with you, that I don't *want* a future with you—"

His face paled. "You don't want a future with me. I know I'm a hard man to like, let alone love, so I understand." He let go of my hand and rose to his feet. "This is why you won't swim with me."

"What?" I gaped up at him from the sofa as I replayed my words in my head. Crap. Too many negatives. No wonder he didn't get it. "I meant I *do* see a future with you." I struggled to my feet. "What can I say? I'm a photographer, not a writer, so I'm not always as eloquent as I want to be. But don't you see? Our future should be *our* decision. Yours and mine, nobody else's. How we want it to look. What it'll mean to both of us. When we decide the time is right. This morning, other people were taking those choices away from us, and it pissed me off. Doesn't that make *you* angry?"

"Aye." There was that scowl, the one I'd come to love. "But only because it upset *you*. I already know"—he pressed his hand on his chest, over where his *calon* lay, and that gold band winked at me, glinting in the light—"*here*, that you're perfect for me, more than Wyn ever was, more than anyone else could ever be."

I rested my hand over his. "How? Some magical fated-mates thingy?"

He chuckled. "There's no such thing as fated mates. But, aye, it's part of a selkie's magic that our hearts recognize the person who'll complete us." He shrugged. "It doesn't always happen to us. Some go their whole lives without a true mate, and for others, they're lucky enough to experience it more than once. Until you, it had never happened to me, that instant certainty." He dipped his chin, gazing at me from under his brows. "But I understand that humans might take longer to know for certain sure."

"You think? It's taken me nearly thirty-seven *years* to get here."

"So...you do want me?" The hope shining in his eyes sent that jolt through me again.

"Of course I want you," I said crossly. "But, for Pete's sake, Lachlan, you never even *asked* me to marry you."

His eyes widened and he blinked. "Is that why you won't swim with me?"

"What does swimming have to do with anything? Listen—" My cell phone rang from my bedroom with the intro to Bryan Ferry's *I Put a Spell on You*, the ringtone I'd assigned to Quest calls. "Sorry. I've got to get that. We're in the middle of a situation with the latest case."

His brows snapped together. "A situation? A dangerous situation? Matthew—"

"Hold that thought." I hurried into the bedroom, nearly landing on my ass when my socks skidded on the floor. I grabbed the phone from the top of the dresser. "Hello?"

"Is ... this ... Mister ... Mann?"

I held the phone away from my ear and frowned at it. The caller ID was Quest, but that voice wasn't Eleri's. "Uh, yes?"

"Please ... hold ... for ... Ms. ... Deilen."

"Hugh?"

"Eleri? Who was that?"

Eleri actually giggled, something I hadn't known she was capable of. "Hector figured out how to rig a voice synthesizer for Miss Pennybaker. She can work the phones now. Isn't that great?"

"Sure, but is it necessary?"

Her sigh was clearly audible. "Yeah, kinda. Zeke still hasn't returned, the selkies are now demanding bubble tea with frog's eggs instead of tapioca, and Paimon is back."

"Paimon? Why? I gave him his proof sheet barely an hour ago."

"He said he's already decided." Her tone held buried mirth. "He wants them all. Multiple copies."

I pinched the bridge of my nose. "Could you please tell him I'll take care of it and let him know when they're ready?"

"I could, I suppose. But he's up in the staff room, keeping our resident spirits in line. Miss Pennybaker's helping me wrangle everything, but it wouldn't be fair for me to leave her alone."

"Everything? You mean there's more?"

The only sound for a moment was a murmur of male voices and a sharp canine yip. Then Eleri sighed. "Yeah. There's been a...development." She must have covered the mouthpiece, because her voice was muffled for a moment before she said, "Mal's at St. Stupid's, following up with the affected patients; Niall's in Faerie, trying to get his brother to broker an agreement with Yannick; Jordan isn't back yet, and I could really use your help."

"I'll be there as soon as I can catch an FTA ride. Oh! Is Hector still there?"

"He is."

"Could you please ask him to contact Jordan and tell him the theft cases can wait? He might have a little trouble reaching him. Lachlan spotted him in the woods above Dewton a while ago. Naked. If he's shifted, he might not be close to his phone." Or perhaps still searching for his clothes. I hoped he remembered that Ted's cave was a safe spot to store things, but I wasn't holding my breath.

"Sure thing, Hugh. See you soon. And *thank you.*"

"You betcha." I disconnected the call and tucked the phone in my pocket.

"Is something amiss?" Lachlan stood in the doorway, carefully not setting foot in my bedroom. *Waiting for permission.*

I really wanted to issue that invitation, but it didn't feel right. Not yet. Until we got our impromptu nuptials sorted out, bedrooms were on hold for us. Unfortunately. So I walked toward the door, and he stood aside to let me pass.

"You could say that." I grabbed my fleece jacket from its hook by the door. "The Quest offices have been invaded."

His eyebrow, the one bisected by a white scar, shot up. "Invaded?"

"Yep." I slung my camera bag over my shoulder. "One conference room is full of selkies—"

"What?" Both brows descended to bunch over his nose. "I warned them to stay well away from you."

I smirked at him. "A royal decree, was it?"

"Shut it," he muttered.

"They, ah, did address me as *Your Highness* the one time I poked my head in the room, but I didn't stay to find out what they wanted."

"They want to be a pain in my arse," he muttered. "I'll come along and have a word with them."

A part of me wanted to refuse, to protest that I could handle my own job, thank you very much. Except the selkies weren't clients, and I really had no idea how to deal with them yet. If Lachlan and I were truly to build a life together, I needed to learn to accept his help.

"Thank you. I'd appreciate that." From the smile he gave me, you'd think I'd just presented him with a Maserati and the keys to an Italian villa. Was I really that prickly about accepting his help? I sighed. Yeah, I probably was. First order of business in married life besides a few days alone together in bed? Learn to accept help gracefully and offer it in return.

Although Lachlan was king of the selkies. What kind of help could I possibly offer him?

I put that aside for the moment, too. "We've got other problems." He followed me onto the porch as I locked up. "Remember that lawsuit?"

"Aye," he growled.

"The Ankou who's suing me has vanished, and as a result, the souls he *should* have escorted on to their final destination are hanging around. Some of them are more...problematic than others."

"Problematic how?" Lachlan asked as we walked, shoulder to shoulder, up the path behind my house that led to the spot where I usually met my FTA driver.

I glanced at him, his features barely visible in the light from the rising moon. "There was...a fatality."

"In your office?"

"No. At the hospital. It seems one of the untethered souls is able to possess others, although not very proficiently."

Lachlan grabbed my arm and turned me to face him on the moonlit path. "Matthew. You mustn't put yourself in danger. If anything should happen to you—"

"Calm down." I patted his chest. "The hopper is targeting supes. It's not going to bother with a human."

"How do you know?"

I tugged on him to get him moving again. "Dr. Mori thinks it's aiming for the most powerful host it can find so it can sort of...reboot its life instead of moving on. In fact"—my grip tightened on his arm and I huddled closer to him—"you might be more in danger than me. After all, you're as big as a mountain and king of the selkies to boot." My middle filled with ice. Dammit, he really was the perfect target if the hopper wanted physical power as well as wealth and influence. I clutched his arm. "Don't come with me. Go back to your boat. Head out to sea. Wait there until we catch this thing."

Lachlan chuckled, cradling my cheek with one big palm. "If you think I'm leaving you to face your troubles alone, you don't know what having a selkie mate means."

I narrowed my eyes. "Does it mean banging my head against a wall every time I tell him to do something for his own good?"

"Perhaps," he said with a lopsided smile. "But it seems having a human mate means much the same."

"I suppose you have a point," I grumbled.

"Matthew." He nudged my chin up so he could kiss me softly. "I'll not get in your way. I'll keep the selkies occupied and let you do your job. You do it well." He kissed me again, then placed a hand on the small of my back and urged me up the hill. "But as you worry for me, I worry for you." He smiled down at me. "Let's keep one another safe, eh?"

My own smile dawned. "I can work with that."

CHAPTER EIGHTEEN

When we got to the clearing in front of Ted's cave, I pulled out one of the oak leaf FTA tokens and pressed my thumb to the rune embossed in gold on its surface. "*Cludo* Frang."

A second later, Frang stepped out from midair. "Hugh." He eyed Lachlan. "Your Majesty."

"Give over, Frang," Lachlan grumbled. "I'm no king of yours, nor anybody else's."

I gazed up at the duergar, who made Lachlan look petite. "Feeling better now? You're not as green as the last time I saw you."

His broad face crumpled, and he actually wrung his hands. "I'm really sorry, Hugh. I had no idea that redcap had hitched a ride."

"No worries, Frang." I gave him my best encouraging smile. "It wasn't your fault."

"But I was the driver. I'm *responsible*." He tugged on the loose collar of his linen shirt as though it were as tight as a noose. "I reported it to the King. He vowed to set spells that'll prevent hitchhiking in the future. I'll comp your ride today. Or this month. Or forever."

"Frang, it's really okay." I patted his arm. "There's no need to give me any special treatment for something that I'm pretty sure couldn't be avoided. Charge me the same as usual." I grinned up at him. "Quest's paying, after all."

"Are you sure?"

"Positive." I gave his arm a final pat. "For now, could you take us along to the Quest offices, please?"

"Sure. But I should warn you…" Frang glanced over his shoulder. "Things are a little weird in Faerie right now."

Considering that Faerie was literally another dimension with a changeable landscape and color spectrum skies, calling it *weird* was, well, weird. "How so?"

He leaned closer. "I feel like I'm being *followed*. But there's never anybody there, not even that redcap."

The hair on my nape prickled. Could the hopper have escaped into Faerie, piggybacked onto one of the other patients in the ER when Dr. Astell had died? AJ didn't think it could survive without possessing a target, but what if he was wrong? Paimon had told me the souls were able to party it up in the Quest staff room because it was steeped in residual magic from its days as a witch's workroom. Faerie was nothing *but* magic. Could the hopper be floating around in there, buoyed by Faerie itself, biding its time until it found the perfect target?

Or—the chill *zing*ed down my spine—could there be more hopper-souls at large and shopping for new bodies?

I chewed my lip, gazing up at Frang. Could he be in danger? He was built like a tank, so from a physical power perspective, he was ideal, but he didn't have a lot of personal influence or wealth. He was essentially a supernatural taxi driver, not exactly a prime target for the power-hungry ex-living. Still…

"Listen, Frang? I don't want to freak you out, but until you get the all-clear from me, maybe only accept fares from people you know, and make sure they keep a good couple of car lengths—er, duergar lengths—away."

His complexion turned as green as when he was on the boat. "You think I *am* being followed? You think it's"—his voice dropped—"*ghosts*?"

I smiled tightly. "Just a precaution for now. You've got Quest's number, right?" He nodded. "If you notice anybody acting strange, promise me you'll give us a call."

He squared his shoulders and set his jaw—although I wasn't entirely sure that wasn't to keep from spewing, since he didn't lose his greenish tinge. "You can count on me, Hugh."

"Good man. Shall we?"

Despite his staunch comment, Frang clearly hadn't conquered his nerves, because he hustled us through Faerie so fast I had to trot to keep up. When we got to the Quest portal, he only lingered until Lachlan and I stepped into the fourth floor corridor before he vanished.

"I hope he'll be okay," I said as I closed the door.

"You've warned him to beware, Matthew." Lachlan kissed the top of my head. "You can do no more for now."

For now. Yeah, that was the issue, wasn't it? *Now* was a total disaster. We needed to find Yannick, like yesterday, and get this situation under control. Slacker Death wasn't the only one who needed to do his freaking job.

"Right. Let's get on with it." I led Lachlan down the hallway. The construction noises hadn't started up again, so I assumed the job site was still closed down upstairs. "I need to check in with Eleri," I said, as we descended to the third floor. "The selkies are in the Little Conference Room. You remember where that is?"

He chuckled. "Aye, I remember. Although I'm not sure your wee building can say the same. It can be as bad as Faerie about keeping things in one place."

I caught his sleeve as we paused on the landing. "I'll check in with you as soon as I can. Be careful?"

"I'll be grand, Matthew. The selkies cannot fash me. I'll send them on their way." He kissed me on the mouth this time and then winked. "Since they insist on calling me king, they've got nobody to blame but themselves if they don't like my orders."

He strode off down the hall, and I might have zoned out a bit, watching his very attractive backside.

Crap. I might not be alone in watching his backside.

I fumbled with the zipper on my camera bag, got the camera strap looped around my neck, and stowed the lens cap. I raised the camera in time to see Lachlan disappear into the LCR to a ragged chorus of *Your Majesty!* from the selkies inside. But once he closed the door, the corridor was clear.

As I trotted down the next flight, I kept the camera at the ready, although I didn't peer through the viewfinder. It would be just my luck to miss a step and tumble down the freaking stairs.

When I walked into the lobby, Eleri was in Zeke's chair, and I picked up Miss Pennybaker on the camera's viewscreen. Did she look...less transparent? She'd taken off her hat, so she'd clearly decided to stay awhile. Her ghostly, parrot-headed umbrella was hanging on an invisible hook on the wall behind her. I wondered briefly whether buildings could be haunted by the shades of renovations past, but then decided it didn't matter. I mean, where else would you hang a transparent umbrella if not on a transparent hook?

Eleri and Miss Pennybaker weren't alone in the lobby. Bryce MacLeod, rocking his usual absent-minded-professor-goes-spelunking vibe, was speaking intently with Tholo, who was nodding along, his expression serious. Hector was standing a little removed from them, his hands in his pockets, shoulders slumped, although he kept casting glances at Bryce and then looking away. Had he come clean to Bryce about his stealth programming, or was he scaring up the courage to confess? From his coiled discomfort, it could be either one.

The tightness in my chest eased slightly because two others were notably absent. "Did Jordan come by to collect Noah and Doop?"

Eleri scrunched up her face. "Nope. That's the situation I was talking about." She pointed to a spot next to her. The desk blocked my view, so I circled around to peer behind it.

Doop was curled into a giant fluffy C and nestled cozily in the curve of his body, sound asleep, was...

"Is that a wolf pup?"

Eleri nodded. "Noah shifted."

"But Jordan's still not back?"

She shook her head, gazing down with a fond smile. "But Doop's doing a great job as doggy nanny until he shows up."

"Ah. Hugh." Bryce strode over to me. "Any update on Yannick Tan's location?"

"No. But Herne's on the trail."

Bryce's eyes narrowed. "Hmmm. Interesting. I hope that doesn't backfire." He reached into one of his vest pockets and pulled out several objects that looked like—

"Scooby-Doo key chains?"

Bryce grimaced. "Yes. Sorry. But they were what I had on hand." When I opened my mouth, he snapped, "Don't ask."

I held up both hands. "Wouldn't dream of it."

He jerked a nod. "Right. Well. The hospital pharmacy witches used loose herbs in linen bags for their protective spells, and while the hospital staff can attach them to their ID lanyards, they're not as easy for others to carry. So my students and I imbued the keychains with the essence of the herbs." He handed one to Eleri, Hector, Tholo, and me. He dangled the last one in his hand. "I didn't expect Noah to be here. I have one for Jordan, but"—he cast a wry glance at the dog pile. "I didn't configure any for use on dog collars."

The Underwood's keys clattered. I half expected the voice synthesizer to kick in, but apparently that only worked on the phone. Eleri leaned over. "Miss Pennybaker says she'll keep any miscreants at bay. The boys are safe with her."

"Good to know." I let my camera rest against my chest so I could hook the key chain's carabiner to my belt loop. "When Herne—"

An anguished cry followed by an angry shout echoed in the stairwell. I went as cold as though I were submerged in the Pacific again, because I recognized both those voices.

Zeke. And Lachlan.

CHAPTER NINETEEN

I tore out of the lobby and up the stairs.

Bryce pounded along at my heels. "Hugh! Wait!"

I paused on the third floor landing long enough to see that nobody was around—neither physical nor incorporeal—at least not until Paimon strode into view.

"Ah, Mr. Mann. If you—"

"Not *now*, Paimon." I swung onto the next flight of stairs, but Bryce grabbed my elbow, sending my camera swinging. I grabbed it before it could collide with the bannister.

"Hugh. Stop. *Think*. You don't know what might be waiting up there."

My heart was pounding so hard it ought to have echoed in the stairwell. "I know this much: Lachlan and Zeke are up there, and they're in trouble."

"I don't dispute that." He shoved his glasses up with one knuckle. "I want to assure their safety too, but not at the expense of perhaps another victim."

Another victim. My fingers were so numb I lost my grip on my camera and it bounced against my chest. Could Lachlan *already* be a victim? Could the hopper have spotted him as the biggest, most powerful, most *precious* person and decided to take over the driver's seat? I couldn't lose him. Not like that. Not ever.

Bryce must have seen that I was about to bolt up the stairs, because his grip tightened. "We'll approach together, Hugh, and with care." His jaw hardened, his eyes going steely. "But not slowly. Come on."

Keeping low, me steadying my camera against my chest so it didn't bang against the stair treads, we raced up the stairs. But when my head cleared floor level and I saw what awaited us, I couldn't hold in a guttural sob.

Because Lachlan was kneeling next to Zeke, who was sprawled on the floor in a scatter of sushi, his broken glasses next to his head. Lachlan's big hands were pressed to Zeke's throat, and he was bloody nearly to his elbows.

"Brodie," Bryce snapped, "what are you doing?"

Lachlan scowled at Bryce and relief washed through me because it was really him—no mere hitchhiker could match that fierce, combative, *wonderful* glare. "Trying to keep the laddie from bleeding out, you wanker. What do you think?"

Bryce turned to me. "Hugh. Quest has an emergency line, right? For staff communications?"

I swallowed hard, my gaze riveted to Zeke's pale face. "Yes."

"Call Mal. Tell him to bring David immediately. Then call Niall." Bryce's gaze flickered to Zeke. "Tell him to bring Hamish." He swallowed. "In case." He knelt on the other side of Zeke's body.

I pulled out my cell phone with one hand to key in the emergency speed dial and lifted my camera with the other. No untethered souls in sight. At least not now.

Mal answered immediately. "What is it, Hugh? I'm a mite busy—"

"Bryce says bring David to Quest immediately. Fourth floor. Zeke's been attacked."

With no hesitation or further questions, he said, "On it."

I keyed in Niall's code, something we'd implemented after our last case when Niall had gone walkabout on us. He picked up at once—he'd promised never to ignore us again. "Hugh? Is something wrong?"

"Yes. Zeke's been injured. Bryce says to bring Hamish. You know." I swallowed again, because my voice was reduced to a croak. "In case."

"David—"

"Mal's bringing him. Quest fourth floor. Hurry."

I returned my attention to the trio on the floor. Zeke's eyes were closed, and he wasn't moving other than the slight movement of his chest as he breathed quick and shallow.

"Did you see what happened?" Bryce's voice was strained. He didn't take his attention from Zeke, and I assumed he was doing some druidy thing to stabilize him as much as possible. "Who attacked him?"

"Nay. I only heard him cry out. He was already on the floor when I rounded that bloody curve." Lachlan jerked his head toward the stairs. "But there's that."

Bryce and I both swung our heads at the same moment. There, leading up to the construction site, was a trail of bloody footprints.

The first two were not human. I'd had enough experience in the supe community to recognize them for what they were: wolf. But three stairs up, they switched to bare human footprints, ball and toe only, as if the person had been running.

"Shit," Bryce muttered, then followed it up with a quick spate of...maybe Gaelic? "I've thrown up a quick shield. The were won't be able to come downstairs, at least for now."

"A werewolf attacked Zeke?" I whispered.

Bryce nodded. "Looks that way. The bite marks on Zeke's neck are unmistakable."

I couldn't take my eyes off Zeke, so still, his blood startlingly bright against his pale skin. "But who would do such a thing?"

"Matthew." Lachlan's tone was gentle. "You know who it had to be."

I stared at him, wide-eyed, my belly tumbling. "You can't mean— *Jordan* would never attack Zeke."

"Aye, Jordan wouldn't. But he's not Jordan any longer."

I shook my head wildly. "No. It can't be. Most of the ER nurses at St. Stupid's are werewolves. They were there when Dr. Astell was killed. It has to be one of them."

"None of them have ever been to Quest. They'd have no call to come here."

My knees buckled and I had to catch myself on the stair rail. This wasn't happening. It couldn't be happening. Zeke was a demon—he was supposed to be indestructible. And Jordan... Jordan wouldn't hurt *anybody*, let alone someone who was a close friend. If Zeke died—

No. I refused to even consider the possibility. David would get here. David could fix almost anything. *But not death.* If a supe's *calon* was extinguished, *achubyddion* had nothing to work with.

But if Jordan *had* done this, even if Zeke recovered—and he *would* recover, dammit—Jordan would still have assaulted another person with apparent intent to kill. Even if we were able to drive the hopper out of Jordan with no residual damage, what kind of punishment could he be facing? What were the legal ramifications when your body attempted to murder somebody when another entity was driving it?

I knew any lawyer trying to present that defense in a *human* court would get slapped down quicker than a lightning strike. But even though I'd nearly been a victim of it myself, there was still a lot I didn't know about *supe* jurisprudence.

The decisive click of boots on the corridor tiles announced Mal's arrival before he strode into view, his broadsword strapped to his back and a paintball tagger holstered at his belt, with David and Ewan hurrying behind him.

As soon as David spotted Zeke, though, he uttered a strangled cry and pushed Mal aside as if my boss didn't have six inches in height on him as well as sporting nearly David's weight in muscle mass. He and Ewan sprinted for Zeke and knelt next to him as SMTs Ky and Pete rattled into sight with a gurney, Zuri winging ahead of them with a squawk of *"Hurry!"*

When a shout heralded the clatter of claws on the stairs, I pushed myself away from the rail to block the stairwell. If not-Jordan intended another try at Zeke, I'd do everything in my power to prevent it. I had my Scooby-Doo key chain, so the hopper couldn't hurt me.

On the other hand, I doubted Scooby was configured to protect me from a werewolf attack. But the canine bounding up the stairs wasn't a possessed werewolf: It was Doop, with wolf-pup Noah frisking along behind him. Hector brought up the rear.

"Sorry, Hugh. I couldn't stop them," he panted.

I pointed at Doop's nose. "Doop. Stop. Stay."

For a moment, I didn't think he'd obey—his eyes were doing that glowy gold thing and his fur bristled along his spine. But when he whined instead of growling, I realized he was worried, not homicidal.

My eyes prickled, and I had to swallow rapidly. If anything were to convince me that Jordan—or at least Jordan's body—was our perp, it was Doop's reaction. Dammit, this could *not* be happening.

But the grim expressions on the medimagical team's faces as they clustered around Zeke, working in near silence, drove home the fact that it was indeed happening. All of it.

Bryce had relinquished his spot at Zeke's side to Ky and gravitated to Mal, who wrapped an arm across his husband's shoulder. I wanted Lachlan's closeness too, but he was on the other side of Zeke, staring down at his bloody hands. No matter how I ached for him, I couldn't abandon my post and risk Doop and Noah following Jordan's trail upstairs.

Because attacking a colleague—even one as beloved as Zeke—was one thing. If not-Jordan attacked Doop, or worse, his own little brother? Even if we got Jordan back, I didn't think he could ever recover from that.

David and Ewan each held one of Zeke's hands, their other hands linked above Zeke's head. Ky murmured, "Can we move him yet? If we could shift him onto the gurney—"

"Zeke!" Hamish bounded down the hallway.

Niall caught up with him, grabbing his arm and swinging him into a full-body hold. "I know you want to go to him, boyo, but you need to let the team work their magic."

Hamish's tortured gaze was riveted on Zeke's pale face. "I can't— Please, can't I hold his hand? Can't I touch him?"

"In a minute," Niall murmured. "Let them move him first." Niall glanced around at the extremely populated landing. "There's not enough room to swing a cat here, let alone a kangaroo."

Niall was right. The corridor was starting to resemble the Rose Quarter MAX stop after a Blazers game.

Pete and Ky lifted Zeke, David and Ewan never releasing his hands, and as they settled him onto the gurney, his eyes fluttered open. "Hamish?" His voice was a thread.

Hamish broke free of Niall and edged closer to the gurney, careful not to disturb David and Ewan. He laid a hand on Zeke's leg. "I'm here, love." The desperate hope and affection in Hamish's broken tone made my knees wobble.

Zeke closed his eyes again. "Good."

Ky smiled at Hamish as Zuri settled on Zeke's chest in a flutter of gray feathers. "We'll take him through the portal to St. Stupid's now, if you'd like to come along."

"Try and stop me," Hamish said with a glare at Niall, who only raised one eyebrow blandly.

Ky and Pete began wheeling the gurney down the hall, David and Ewan crab-walking at its head and Hamish bringing up the rear with his hand never leaving Zeke's leg. Suddenly, they stopped, and my heart stuttered. Had Zeke taken a turn for the worse?

When I spotted the antlers brushing the ceiling beyond the little group, I blew out a relieved breath. They'd only hit a meta-god roadblock.

"Excuse me," Ky said. "Coming through."

Herne inclined his head and moved aside, and as the gurney parade passed him, I noticed that his hand gripped the shoulder of none other than Slacker Death.

Yannick watched the group wheel Zeke past, his mouth hanging open. Even when Herne jerked him into a stumbling walk toward us, he kept his head cranked around to watch them.

"Wh-what happened to him?" Then he saw the blood puddle on the floor. "Did somebody *die*?"

My jaw clenched, my ears heating so fast they probably smoked. I powered past Bryce, Mal, Niall—even Lachlan—in my need to get at Yannick Tan. Lachlan's hand—still red with Zeke's blood—on my shoulder stopped me from launching my fist at Yannick's face.

"No thanks to you." I jerked my shoulder out of Lachlan's grip. "You're pretty damn squeamish for a guy who's the personification of Death!"

"I don't *kill* anybody." Yannick's self-righteous tone made me want to hit him even more. He pointed to Herne. "That's *his* job."

"If you'd done *your* job, *this*"—I jabbed my finger at the aftermath of Zeke's attack—"would never have happened. One of the souls you bailed on has been possessing innocent victims. *Using* their bodies. *Killing* them. Nearly killing others."

"That's not my fault," he said sullenly. "If you hadn't—"

"Oh no." I got right up in his face. "You are not laying this on me. You have *one job*. And you *didn't do it*. Where the hell have you been, anyway?"

His gaze shifted away from me. "Nowhere."

"Yannick." I loaded my tone with as much threat as I could. "Where. Have. You. Been?"

He glared at me. "At a Comic-Con, okay? They were giving away *Yuri on Ice* T-shirts."

"I don't believe this," I muttered, running a hand through my hair. "Okay. Here's the deal. The entity that did this"—I gestured to the floor although I couldn't look at it myself without my stomach trying to rebel—"is probably upstairs right now."

His eyes nearly bugged out. "It's *here*?" he squeaked.

"Where else could it be, since you've been off scrounging anime swag? You're going to go up there and take custody of it right freaking now and escort it to whatever limbo it belongs in, preferably somewhere with zero amenities and hot and cold running torment, and, I don't know, *bedbugs*. And you're doing it *now*."

"B-but it's violent," he whined. "The souls I escort are never violent."

"Maybe because you never made them wait this long before."

"I—I can't. What if it goes for me??

"Oh, for Pete's sake." I unhooked Scooby from my belt loop and thrust it at him. "This'll keep it from possessing you. And since we've got a mountain-sized selkie, two fae warriors, a druid, a werewolf, and Herne the freaking Hunter here, I think you're safe from any physical attacks. Now go."

From the way Yannick's gaze flicked right and left, I could tell he was considering making a break for it. I had no idea whether he could escape without a fixed portal, but he was clearly assessing his options.

"Don't even think about it, dude," I said. "The jig is most definitely up. You're doing this. Now. Get it?"

Yannick huffed out a breath as he adjusted his ball cap. "Got it."

I bared my teeth at him. "Good."

He glared at me. "But I'm still not—"

"A party? And nobody invited me?" Paimon strolled up, his hair flames leaping merrily. He stuck out his lower lip. "I'm beginning to think you don't *like* me, Hugh. You have no idea how that hurts my feelings."

CHAPTER
TWENTY

My fists curled, but I forced them to unclench, because punching the Auditor General of hell was a really bad idea. "Paimon. Please. *Not now.*"

"But you're such a difficult man to pin down. I really need to get these headshots done. I've gotten masses of requests for them from my fans."

"I'm sorry, but we're trying to capture that hopper-soul." I gestured to Yannick. "Now that we've got a psychopomp."

Paimon eyed Yannick. "Not a very prepossessing specimen."

"Hey!" Yannick straightened in an attempt at swagger. "I'm very prepossessing."

"You better be good at *un*possessing, because that's what you're about to do." I grabbed his elbow. "Come on." I hauled Yannick toward the stairs, but Lachlan stepped into my path.

"Matthew. You can't go up there." He started to reach for me, but winced at the blood drying on his hands and dropped his arms to his sides. "Humans have no defense against possession or werewolf attack."

Hector gasped, his eyes widening. "Werewolf? That— One of *us* did that? Is it somebody I know?"

My gaze skittered away from his pleading face. "Remains to be seen. For now, just"—I gestured down the hallway with the hand not holding onto Yannick—"take Doop and Noah over there and hang out, okay?"

Hector nodded and scooped Noah up, tucking him under one arm despite the kid's—pup's?—protesting yip. He gripped Doop's ruff and edged past Mal and Bryce as I faced Lachlan.

"Sweetheart, I'm not brainless. *I'm* not going up there." I waggled Yannick's elbow. "*He* is. You're in more danger than I am because you're the only one here without a protective charm." I frowned. "At least I *think* you are."

Bryce jerked a nod. "Everyone else is covered." He glanced sidelong at Paimon and Herne. "Except them."

Paimon waved one hand airily. "Oh, nobody can possess *me*." He waggled his eyebrows. "Although many have tried."

Herne crossed his arms. "I am likewise immune."

Bryce held up another Scooby key chain. "I've got one more of these. It was for—" He swallowed, his eyes bleak, and I remembered he was one of Jordan's teachers, maybe as close to the young werewolf as we were here at Quest. "—another of your gang." He tossed the key chain at Lachlan, who caught it easily. "Keep that on you and you're covered, Brodie."

Lachlan tried to press it on me. "You take it, Matthew."

I pushed his hand away. "No way. If the hopper is seeking power or riches, you're the most tempting target here, because you've got both."

His scowl deepened. "I don't like it."

"Will it make you feel better if I put you in charge of Yannick?"

I don't know if I've mentioned it, but under certain circumstances, when he isn't scowling, Lachlan can boast a grin that's a perfect blend of gleeful and feral. He turned it on Yannick, who cowered against me with a whimper.

"Aye," Lachlan said. "That'll do nicely."

I leaned over and mock whispered to Yannick, "Pro tip? He's my boyfriend, and he's already peeved at you for suing me, so don't piss him off anymore."

Lachlan took Yannick's arm, and from the Ankou's wince, he wasn't particularly gentle. Which, if I'm being honest, I wasn't sorry about in the least. Mal and Niall flanked them, both with their swords out. My insides froze again, because this could be *Jordan*.

Unless, of course, it wasn't anymore.

I buried my reaction as best I could and joined Hector and the canine contingent as Bryce took up the rear position with Mal's paintball tagger. And before you wonder why Mal would bring what amounted to a toy to a possibly lethal confrontation, Bryce had druidified the paintball charges with an anti-evil potion. I kind of wanted to suggest that he go first, but I knew Mal would never allow it. He was just as protective of his husband as Lachlan was of me.

Which...bore thinking about at some other time.

"They won't hurt him, will they?" Hector murmured. I realized he didn't know the attacker could be Jordan. I decided not to bring up that particular detail.

"They'll do their best."

Hector frowned. "That's not very reassuring, Hugh."

"What can I tell you? That's all I've got. It's all up to Yannick now." And *that* didn't fill me with confidence. Slacker Death hadn't shown me any evidence that he could do anything other than vanish when things got difficult.

"Drop the shields, Bryce," Mal said.

Bryce made a gesture and murmured another Gaelic phrase. "Done."

The group moved up the stairs, Yannick clearly dragging his feet. They reached the landing halfway up, where the flight made a U-turn.

I craned my neck, but the hallway ceiling blocked my view. "See anything?"

"Stay back, Matthew," Lachlan growled. "You'll know when we— Shite!"

I didn't need to ask why he was cursing—I heard the low, rumbling growl. Doop heard it too, because his hackles went all the way up and his ears all the way down. Next to me, he radiated cold like a block of dry ice, a sure sign that he was stressed or angry, since ordinarily he was merely icepack chilly.

The group froze on the landing, making it extremely crowded, because three of the five guys up there were super-sized and one was at least extra-large. Yannick, the only medium-to-small guy, stared up at the head of the stairs, his eyes nearly bugging out.

"Do something," I hissed. What was he waiting for?

"It's— It's *anchored* itself," he croaked. "I don't know—"

"Then cut the anchor rope, you wanker," Lachlan growled, "and do your job."

A gray wolf, its size marking it as a were and not an ordinary wolf, began creeping down the stairs, belly fur brushing the treads. I held onto a dim hope that it was some *other* werewolf until I saw the telltale white blaze on his flank.

"Is that *Jordan*?" Hector croaked.

"I'm afraid so."

"Did he do"—Hector gestured vaguely at the blood pooled on the tiles—"that?"

I nodded grimly. "Looks like it."

"They can't— They won't *hurt* him, will they?" He gazed at me, despair in his dark eyes. "Not Jordan."

I gripped Hector's shoulder. "Not if they can help it."

"Is there anything I can do? We're pack. Maybe if I talk to him, he'll—"

"The best thing we can do right now is stay here and let those guys do their job."

"But—"

With a sound halfway between growl and bark, Doop charged past us, knocking both Hector and me off balance. My arms flailed as I tried to stay on my feet.

Mistake.

I should have tackled Noah instead, because the pup followed Doop, and the two of them charged up several steps toward the landing.

"Herne," Niall barked, "get them away."

"They do not answer to me," Herne replied, although he strode past Paimon and approached the stairs.

"Doop!" I called. "Here, boy."

Doop ignored me. His glowing yellow eyes were fixed on Jordan—or rather Jordan's wolf with somebody else in the driver's seat. In their glow, the shadow of the stair railings swung against the wall as he crept upward. Noah's claws scrabbled on the wooden treads as he emerged from under Doop's belly and scrambled up another step.

"Noah, no!" I darted forward, but my feet skidded on—*not thinking about that*—and I had to grab my camera as it swung sideways.

"Stay *back*, Matthew," Lachlan roared.

Noah whined, whether at Lachlan's shout or because he was picking up the tension in the situation, but it caught not-Jordan's attention and his gaze snapped from the group on the landing to Doop and Noah. His wolfy lips drew away from his *extremely* sharp teeth in a parody of a grin, and I noticed that the fur on his muzzle was matted with dried blood. *Zeke's blood.*

"Yannick," Mal shouted. "Get off your bloody arse and do your job."

To absolutely nobody's shock, Yannick did nothing.

With a muttered curse, Bryce aimed the paintball tagger, but just as he got his shot off, not-Jordan leaped.

Not toward Yannick or Lachlan or Bryce. No. He leaped *over the freaking railing*, straight at Noah and Doop. The anti-evil paintball splattered harmlessly against the wall.

"No!" I cried. But before I could move, not-Jordan's body twisted awkwardly in the air, hind legs torquing one way, head and forelegs in the opposite direction, and a loud *crack* echoed in the stairwell. The wolf crashed to the stairs in front of Doop's nose.

"Oh, God." I staggered sideways until my shoulder slammed into the wall. My camera, usually the thing that grounded me, no matter what, was a foreign lump in my hands, alien and sinister and merciless. I glared at the men on the stairs, strangers in my blurry vision. "Did you do that? Without even *trying* to talk to him?"

"Hugh." Bryce's voice cut into me, not because it was sharp or angry, but because it wasn't.

I looked down, so I wouldn't see if his expression, if all their expressions, held the same sorrow and regret. And my gaze caught on the camera's viewscreen and my fingers went numb.

Something was happening.

I pushed myself off the wall. Of course something was happening. With its host—I had to swallow against the howl that threatened to burst out of my throat—*gone*, the hopper would need another target. And with everybody protected and nobody to hop to, to hide inside, Yannick could finally grab it. I held my camera up and pointed it toward—I swallowed again —Jordan's body. If I could track the hopper's movements, I could at least warn everyone where it was headed.

I could do that much for him.

A gray mist formed over Jordan, amorphous at first but then coalescing into the translucent figure of an untethered soul.

I squinted, certain I couldn't be seeing this right. But then the figure turned and glared at me with such hatred and malice that I couldn't be mistaken. "Uh, guys?" I croaked. "The hopper-soul is—"

It rushed me, jaw unhinged and gaping wider, wider, wider, and then it—

CHAPTER
TWENTY-ONE

Someone was running their fingers through my hair, stroking my beard, kissing my forehead.

"Mmmm," I murmured. "That's nice."

"Matthew? Oh, thank the sea."

And suddenly I was being suffocated against what felt like a flannel-covered brick wall.

"Mmmph!" I flailed for an instant before I could breathe again.

More stroking. "I'm sorry, *mo cridhe.*"

Mo cridhe. Oh! I cracked my eyes open to see Lachlan's dear face peering down at me, his wavy mane back-lit by fluorescent ceiling lights. The telltale beep of medical equipment and the combined scents of herbs and antiseptic meant I had to be in the St. Stupid's ER. Again.

Then I remembered. The hopper-soul. Zeke. *Jordan.*

I fisted Lachlan's shirt. "Are they okay? Zeke? Jordan?"

Lachlan smoothed my hair off my—*ewww*—sweaty forehead. "Alive."

I narrowed my eyes. "That doesn't answer my question."

"Aye, well, that's the best I can do. Zeke's faring better than young Jordan, but then, his attack was only physical. Jordan's... well, the beastie was in him for a good while."

"A bad while is more like it." I let go of Lachlan's shirt and fell back against the hospital's poor excuse for a pillow. "It killed Dr. Astell, and it was in Jordan for much longer. How did he survive?"

He shrugged one shoulder. "The laddie is strong, *mo cridhe*. AJ and Dr. Kendrick think he withstood the possession better because his soul is pure and his heart is true."

I swallowed thickly. "I saw it, Lachlan. When it rose out of Jordan. It was—"

"Athaniel. Aye, we ken that now."

"Is he—"

"Gone. For good this time."

"Yannick finally did his job?"

Lachlan's mouth twisted in disgust. "Nay. 'Twas Paimon. He said the only way to truly banish a member of the Host is to dismantle their manifestation matrix. He, ah, took care of it himself. With extreme prejudice."

I plucked at the edge of my blanket, not meeting Lachlan's gaze. "I should have seen it sooner. AJ told us that only a member of the Host could possess others. If I'd suspected Athaniel in the first place, we—"

"Matthew." Lachlan captured my hands. "You cannot take this onto your shoulders."

I frowned at his big, tanned hands, the calluses on his palms rough against my fingers. "Sure I can."

"No. You cannot."

I glared up at him. He was smiling fondly at me, which amped my frown up another seven or thirteen or forty-three notches. "Why?"

"Because it is not your fault. And I will not let you." He raised my hands and kissed both palms. "You were not the only one who missed the clues, nor are you the only one trying to take the blame." His eyes glinted with amusement. "Paimon went so far as to apologize for losing track of his...what did he call it? His little personnel problem." He chuckled. "From what he tells us, Athaniel was astonished at his fate right up until his matrix collapsed and he dissipated for good."

"No surprise there." I smiled wearily. "He never believed that angels and demons were built from the same blueprints."

"Aye, well, he always was a wanker."

I remembered the monstrous transformation of Athaniel's features as he rushed at me. "Wait." I patted myself down—face, chest, belly. "Did he *possess* me? Did I do anything? Did I *hurt* anybody?"

"Relax, *mo cridhe*." Lachlan pressed a soft kiss to my forehead. "He tried. But he failed."

"Failed? How? I was the only person there without a protective charm."

"Ah, but you had a charm of your own." He touched the center of my chest. "God-touched, remember?"

"Really?" When Lachlan nodded, my hand crept up to the spot where Govannon had laid the tip of his ginormous finger against me for, like, an instant. I hadn't thought much more about it. Niall had told me it left a magical residue, but he'd made it sound like it was a disadvantage more than a benefit, making me more desirable as a spell ingredient for unscrupulous magic users. I hadn't expected it to act like a force field instead, but thank goodness it had.

The last thing I wanted was Athaniel's slimy consciousness slithering around inside my head.

God, Jordan had had that for hours. I clutched Lachlan's hands. "Jordan. He must be devastated. Does he know what he did? You know, during the possession?"

Lachlan sighed. "Much of it, aye. AJ says the memories left behind after a possession can vary. Since Athaniel wasn't adept at possession, his attempts were more brute force than finesse. So they rattled the victims' brains a bit."

"Mental blunt force trauma?"

"Aye. That's why you passed out." He mock glared at me, making me shiver. "Don't frighten me like that again, Matthew, I'm begging you."

I chuckled weakly. "I always *try* to keep the near-death experiences to a minimum." Then I took a deep, steadying breath, because there was one death—Death-with-a-capital-D—that I needed to get near at least one more time. "Where's Yannick?"

Lachlan laughed, shaking his head. "I know that look. It's your determined-investigator face."

I blinked at him. "I have a determined-investigator face?"

"Aye." He waggled his eyebrows. "Very fetching. It's one of the things that drew me to you at the very first. I could tell you were a man who wanted to make a difference, to do the right thing." He cupped my cheek. "I wasn't wrong."

Heat rushed up my throat, and I wondered whether the beeping monitors next to me would record a spike in temperature or a change in blood pressure. If so, how embarrassing. The sooner I lost the medical polygraph equipment, the better.

I waggled the pulse oximeter clamped on my index finger. "When can I get sprung from this place?"

"As soon as Dr. Mori signs off on your discharge. AJ came by and verified you weren't possessed, so they don't need to keep you around for observation."

"Good. That's good." I wasn't in a hospital johnny, so at least I didn't have to change. "I want to talk to Yannick, but I'd like to see Zeke and Jordan before I go."

"Hamish is sitting with Zeke. Hasn't left his side for a moment, but I expect he'd let you drop by for a wee visit."

"And Jordan?"

Lachlan winced. "That may be a mite trickier. He's not wanting to see anybody right now. AJ says that's typical, since if a target remembers their actions during a possession, they're likely to blame themselves. Think they should have done better, been stronger. But he also says that's impossible. Once the possession takes hold, the Host is in charge."

I frowned. "But that's not— At the last, when Athaniel lunged for Doop and Noah and fell mid-leap? Bryce said none of our hopper-soul emergency response team was responsible, so that had to be Jordan taking control. No way would Athaniel volunteer for pain or denial for the sake of anybody else."

"Aye. And Dr. Mori's in no hurry to let the laddie go before she finds out why that happened."

I gazed at him. He wasn't going to like my next request. Like at all. So I kissed his palm first before smiling at him in a way that I hoped was beguiling. Given the way his eyebrows snapped together, I needed to work on my subterfuge.

He peered at me through narrowed eyes. "What?"

"I know you're in full-on overprotective juggernaut mode at the moment—"

"You could have been killed!"

I kissed his palm again. "But I'm fine now. I'm in a hospital. What could happen?" I hid my wince, because the last time I'd said that, a whole crap-ton of stuff had happened. "I'd like to have the next few conversations in private, though. Would you please wait for me at my place? I'll join you there as soon as I'm done."

He scowled—and yeah, that was really starting to do it for me in a big way. "I don't like it."

"I know. But it's important. Please, Lachlan?"

For a moment, I thought he'd refuse. But then he nodded with a sigh. "Aye. If that's what you want, *mo cridhe*."

I was about to pull him down into a kiss with a little more intent—both gratitude and promise—when the curtain rattled and Renee bustled in, smiling widely at me. "Mr. Mann, as much as we love you here, we sincerely hope you won't be back again today."

"Trust me, Renee," I pushed myself up to sit on the edge of the gurney, Lachlan's big, warm hand steady on my back. "Nobody wishes for that more than I do." I met her gaze squarely. "But before I go, could you do me a favor?"

CHAPTER
TWENTY-TWO

"Hugh!" Zeke beamed at me from his bed. Its head was cranked far enough that he was almost sitting upright. Hamish, as Lachlan had said, was sitting in a chair snugged up against the bed, holding Zeke's hand. "You're okay! They told me that Athaniel attacked you, too."

"He tried." I tapped my head. "Rebounded off my thick skull, so no harm done." I walked to his bedside. "You're the one we were worried about."

He waved my words away, his blush blotching his face. "Oh, I'm fine. David and Ewan fixed me up. I'm not sure why they won't let me go back to work. The office must be in an uproar."

"Because you nearly bled out, love." Hamish's exasperated tone hinted that he'd had this argument with Zeke more than once. "The office can manage without you for a bit."

I nodded. "It's true. Between Eleri and Miss Pennybaker, with a little tech help from Hector, they've got things covered."

His eyebrows rose. "Miss Pennybaker is still there?"

"Uh…" I hadn't actually been back to the office yet. "She was the last time I was." Which was also the last time Zeke was there, but I didn't want to dwell on that—Hamish still looked like he was ready to tuck Zeke in his pocket and take him away. However, if Yannick was back on the job, Miss Pennybaker might not be there much longer, if she was still there at all. Of course, it was still a huge question about whether Yannick *was* back on the job. He might still be slacking off—which was definitely the option that had my bet. "Don't worry. We'll be fine."

"See?" Hamish twined one of Zeke's dark curls around his finger. "They'll be grand while I take you on a little vacation."

Zeke's eyes grew round behind his glasses. "A vacation? Where?"

"Disneyland."

"Oh," Zeke breathed, "I've always wanted to go there."

"I know," Hamish said, his smile doting. And since Zeke's smile in return was equally affectionate, I decided it was time for me to go.

"Take care, Zeke. Hope you both have a great time on your trip."

I don't think they even noticed when I left. Renee met me in the hallway. She winked. "Everything's ready and waiting for you upstairs. He's in room 412."

I took the stairs, just because I could. Nothing like nearly getting booted out of your body to make you appreciate it in all its imperfections. When I reached Jordan's room, Dr. Kendrick was standing outside, his hands clasped behind his back. He nodded at me. "Hugh."

I peeked past his broad shoulders through the sidelight next to the door. Jordan was lying on his side, facing away from us. "Have his parents come?"

Dr. Kendrick's noble jaw tightened. He was just as beautiful as both his brothers, although Mal's beauty was rougher and Gareth's wilder. The eldest Kendrick could only be described as austere, but I'd glimpsed his softer side whenever he gazed at his husband. "No."

I frowned. "But—"

"They remain unresponsive to all attempts to reach them, even when the call came from the Queen herself."

"Jerks," I muttered.

Dr. Kendrick's lips twitched. "Just so."

"What about Tanner? Chase? The other Dog House guys?"

"They came, but he wouldn't see them. And Tanner isn't the type of alpha to force a confrontation, so they left him in peace." He sighed. "Although I'm not certain that was the best strategy."

"What do you mean?"

Beyond the window, Jordan stirred, rolling onto his back. Dr. Kendrick drew me away so he wouldn't see us watching him through the sidelight like he was an exhibit in a zoo. "Like most weres, Jordan craves connection, the closeness of pack. But unlike his parents, who are willing to shirk what should be their most sacred duty—that of parent to child—Jordan also craves involvement. Occupation. Engagement. I don't think leaving him alone will promote his recovery, because it's not what he truly wants." He smiled at me. "Therefore, I think your plan is ideal." He raised one perfect eyebrow, and for an instant, he resembled Mal at his cheekiest. "As good as any treatment I could devise myself." He gestured to the door. "Please carry on."

I nodded once, straightened my shoulders and marched toward the door. My courage failed before I actually crossed the threshold, though—I'd give Jordan that much choice, anyway. So I paused in the doorway and rapped on the frame. "Hey, buddy. Mind if I come in?"

"Hugh?" Jordan's breath hiccupped, and he wiped his wet cheeks with both hands. "What are you doing here?"

I crossed to the bed. "One of my team was injured on the job. What kind of leader would I be if I didn't check on him?"

He turned his head away. "I don't deserve to be on the team." His voice was low, as though he were talking to himself and not to me.

"Hey! My team, so I get to decide who deserves to be on it." I grasped his wrist where it lay atop the pale blue blanket. "And I'm pretty sure my team can't function without you."

He turned back to me, tears leaking from his red-rimmed eyes. "But I hurt Zeke, Hugh. I almost *killed* him."

I tightened my grip on his wrist a fraction. "No, Jordan. *You* didn't. Athaniel did."

"But I couldn't stop him," Jordan murmured brokenly. He tugged his hand from my grip and pounded on the blanket in time with his words. The monitors next to the bed began beeping faster. "Couldn't shake him. I tried, Hugh! I promise I tried."

"Shhh. I know." I captured his hand again, patting it in an attempt to soothe him. "You did great."

"I didn't, though." His face crumpled. "Zeke's blood, Hugh. In *my* mouth. My wolf's mouth. I can't—" He dashed his free hand under his eyes. "And then he wanted to kill Noah. And Doop. If he'd managed—"

"He didn't. Hell, Jordan, you snapped your own spine to stop him. That took serious courage and determination." I smiled, trying to scare a ghost of his former grin out of him. "You're a hero."

He shook his head. "I should have done better. I should never have let him in to begin with."

"I doubt you could have stopped him," I said dryly. "You had no idea what he was or what he wanted. And that's on me. On me and everybody else who missed all the signs. I'm sorry, Jordan. I'm sorry we allowed you to be put in harm's way."

"I doubt you could have stopped him." Jordan echoed my words and finally met my gaze, his eyes haunted. "He *hated* us, Hugh."

"Well, he's always believed that angels were better than everyone and entitled to behave any way they wished."

"No, I don't mean he hated people in general. He hated *us*. Zeke. You. Me. Doop. He *wanted* to kill us. To make us suffer."

I considered that for a moment. "He was Zeke's AI—his angel interface watchdog—back before the Realm Accords. Since the upshot of that situation was him getting sentenced to Sheol and

Govannon's forge, I can see how he could have blamed Zeke." I rolled my eyes. "Because god knows it couldn't have been his own fault. Then, when he'd come up with a scam to escape that fate, Doop and I headed him off at the pass." I poked Jordan's side gently. "And you broke his nose with a Frisbee. Considering how vain he is, that may have been the unkindest cut of all."

He scowled at me, picking at his blanket. "That's not funny, Hugh."

I sighed. "I'm sorry. And I know this isn't something you'll be able to shake off quickly." I leaned forward. "You were violated, Jordan. He used you against your will, and that's a big deal. A huge deal. But you've got people here to help you, for as long as it takes you to feel better. Me. Eleri. Mal, Niall, and Zeke."

He gave a watery scoff. "Not Zeke. He couldn't."

"Zeke especially. Nobody knows Athaniel's cruelty and pettiness better than he does. He's already forgiven you. And Dr. Kendrick said he'll clear his calendar whenever you want to talk with him."

"Maybe later."

From his tone, I doubted he'd be volunteering for that any time soon. Time to put my plan into action. "But there are a couple of folks who won't wait any longer."

He looked up, panic chasing across his face. Oh yeah. He knew what I was about to spring on him. "I don't want to—"

"Please, Jordan." Time to play dirty for his own good. "If not for you"—I gave him my own version of puppy-dog eyes— "then for them."

He exhaled, long and shakily, but nodded at last, so I rose and crossed to the door. When I opened it, Doop charged in, yipping excitedly. Noah, still in wolf pup form, gamboled along behind him. With a flying leap, Doop landed on the bed—which had to be sturdier than it looked, because it barely wobbled. He managed to land with his paws braced alongside Jordan's body rather than on top of him, which I chalked up to hellhound magic.

He nosed Jordan's chin until Jordan finally buried his hands in Doop's ruff with a wobbly smile. "Hey, boy."

Meanwhile, Noah, front paws on the mattress, was hopping on his back feet, trying vainly to climb onto the bed. With a muffled sob, Jordan held out his arms, so I picked Noah up and handed him to his big brother. Jordan buried his face in Noah's fur, and his shoulders shook as the wolf pup tried to lick his face. Unfortunately for Noah, he only succeeding in getting a mouthful of hair.

"He's going to need your help, Jordan," I said softly. "You're the only person in your family responsible enough to guide him out of his first shift."

Jordan's shoulders shook harder, but from Noah's indignant squeak and Doop's contented huff, he was holding on to them as fiercely as they held onto him.

I crept out of the room, leaving the family reunion to continue in peace. When I closed the door, Renee was there. "Is there anything they need?" Her voice wobbled a little. Well, she was a werewolf too. She probably understood what they were going through better than anybody.

I glanced through the sidelight into the room, a smile dawning. "Do you think you could send an orderly out for some Frisbees?"

She grinned. "I think that could be arranged."

"Great." I glanced back again. Doop had stretched out on the bed on Jordan's left and Noah was tucked under his right arm.

Dr. Kendrick joined me. "Excellent work, Hugh."

I sighed. "You really think I did the right thing?"

He nodded, flicking a finger at the puppy pile on the bed. "He'll be strong for them. An alpha always rises to the occasion when his pack is in need."

CHAPTER
TWENTY-THREE

Despite my unintentional nap—although technically it was lack of consciousness more than actual sleep—my eyes were gritty and my limbs leaden. But this extremely long day wasn't over yet, so after I left Dr. Kendrick outside Jordan's room, I cadged a cup of truly dreadful hospital coffee from Renee and collected my camera bag from the nurse's station.

Ordinarily, I'd just take human-style transportation back to Quest. I preferred to save my FTA tokens for longer trips, and St. Stupid's in Northeast Portland wasn't that far from our offices in the Pearl district. I could easily climb on a MAX train, hop a bus, or call up a ride share of some kind.

But today I had business in Faerie.

So after I left Jordan's room, I trudged down the stairs to St. Stupid's translocation portal and fished out my last FTA token. I pressed the rune. "*Cludo* Frang."

Frang immediately stepped out of the portal's amorphous swirl, but from the tension in his shoulders and the way he glanced furtively around the antechamber, he was still freaked out. "Hugh? Why are you at the hospital? You never call me from the hospital."

"I know. I just wanted to talk to you."

His eyes widened, an expression of near wonder softening his craggy features. "Me? Really?"

"Yep." I gestured to the portal. "Walk with me?" As long as I remained ambulatory anyway—Renee's caffeinated sludge wouldn't last forever. "Back to the office?"

"Sure thing, Hugh."

He led me across the threshold. With my first long, indrawn breath, the air in Faerie—wild and untamed, scented with pine and wood smoke and a dizzying sweetness that Eleri said was the One Tree in bloom—eased the tightness in my chest and the ache at the base of my skull, revitalizing me. Not completely— I'm not sure even Faerie has *that* kind of magic—so I was still dog-tired. But enough that I could do what needed to be done.

Frang matched his stride to mine as we trod the path next to the water—a burbling creek today rather than a raging torrent. "Um. Nice weather we're having?"

I laughed. Frang was worse at small talk than Herne. "Don't worry, Frang. I don't expect you to carry the conversational ball." I glanced up at him. "Remember my warning?"

"About only accepting fares from people I know? Yeah."

"I wanted to let you know that the primary danger has passed. So you don't need to worry about that anymore. You should be able to return to your usual routine."

"Oh."

Oookaaay. That wasn't relief in Frang's tone. I dodged ahead and turned to face him, blocking the path. "Is something else wrong?"

He glanced over his shoulders, twice on each side, before bending down toward me and whispering, "I still feel like I'm being followed. There's a…a *presence*."

I frowned. "A malevolent presence? Do you feel threatened?"

He shrugged one massive shoulder. "No? I don't know. It's just…weird."

Blame the slow uptake on my lack of sleep, but I finally got it. "Frang, can I take your picture?"

He blinked. "My picture? Why?"

"Humor me, okay? I've got an idea, but I'm running on fumes right now, so it might come to nothing."

He nodded, so I unzipped my bag. I gazed down at my camera, which had been almost another body part for most of my adult life. The last time I'd held it...I swallowed hard, my fingers hovering above its sleek black frame. Would I still be *me* if my camera felt as alien in my hands as when I'd held it last, with Zeke's blood on the floor, Jordan's broken body on the stairs, and Athaniel roaring toward me with his jaws gaping?

I almost closed the bag again, because, you know, denial works *so* well. But Frang was peering down at me in between glances over his shoulders. To ease his discomfort, I had to face my own. So I took a deep breath, set my jaw, and drew the camera out of its padded nest.

I nearly crumpled onto the path when it settled in my hand like the old friend it was, muscle memory taking over as I stowed the lens cap, one hand cradling the long lens as I raised the camera and peered through the viewfinder.

As I suspected, Frang and I weren't alone on the path. A semi-transparent duergar was hovering behind Frang—and wow. Either there wasn't a lot of genetic diversity in duergars as a species, or this one was closely related to Frang, right down to the same clothing choices. I snapped the shot, which caused the unknown duergar's eyes to widen in an expression exactly like Frang's when he was freaked out about Doop.

I turned the camera to show Frang the viewscreen. "Do you know this person?"

Frang's jaw dropped. He blinked rapidly, one tear escaping to zigzag its way to his chin. "Th-that's my cousin Mungo. He's been gone for over a century."

"He didn't happen to make a deal with a demon, did he?"

Frang whirled to face the air where Mungo had been in the shot. "Mungo, you...you..." He aimed a punch at the air, which, of course, didn't land. "Is *that* how you beat me in that dice game? You sold your soul?" He turned his back and crossed his arms. "I should have known. There's no way you could have won. You're a terrible player."

I kept my eye on the viewscreen. Mungo looked suitably chastened as he tried to pat Frang's arm—which also failed to connect. "The thing is, a lot of contracted souls were released from Sheol recently, but the Ankou who was supposed to escort them onward fell down on the job in a major way." I circled Frang so I could look up into his face. "But we've got him back on track now." Or we would, and pretty dang quick. "If you like, I can ask him to put Mungo at the top of the list."

"What?" Frang uncrossed his arms and grabbed my shoulder. "No! I don't want him to go." In the viewscreen, Mungo grinned and attempted to hug Frang, only to succeed in passing right through him—and me. "Now that I know it's him, I don't mind being followed." He smiled a little shyly. "It's kinda nice not being alone, you know?"

I replaced the lens cap and stowed the camera in the bag, taking more time than I needed with the zipper. "You know, Frang, if Mungo wants to move on, it should be his decision."

Frang sighed, his shoulders rising nearly a foot before they fell. "I get it. But for as long as he wants to stay, I'm glad he's with me." He sniffed. "I've missed him. Even if he cheated at dice."

Frang turned chattier than I'd ever known him to be for the rest of our trip, sometimes addressing comments to me about Mungo, and sometimes addressing Mungo himself. It didn't seem to matter to him whether Mungo answered or not. He waved at me cheerily when we reached the freestanding door that led to Quest. Without my camera, I couldn't be certain, but I suspected that Mungo did the same.

When I stepped through the portal, the whine of a saw and hammers banging in uncoordinated counterpoint clued me in that construction had resumed in Zeke's old apartment. I winced, hoping that there wasn't any residual...evidence of Athaniel's crimes remaining. However, my bosses knew what they were doing, so they'd probably gotten everything ritually cleansed before they'd allowed Rusty's crew back on site.

Did they have a spell to ritually cleanse *us* of this *extremely* long day's events? Because if not, I wasn't sure our new staff lounge would ever be used by, you know, staff.

As I reached the stairs, I avoided looking too closely at the place where Zeke had lain. A quick peek showed the tiles were pristine and gleaming as only a brownie cleaning service could manage. So maybe we were back to business as usual? Or maybe we were just really good at pretending.

I sidled onto the stairs and trotted down. If Lachlan had done as I asked, he'd be waiting for me back at my house. We definitely needed to talk, but before I could truly concentrate on him and what I wanted to say, I needed to clear the decks here first.

As soon as I walked into the lobby, Eleri shrieked, "Hugh!" She leaped out of the chair behind the desk and raced across the room to fling herself at me. "You're okay!"

I had to catch my balance so both of us didn't topple onto the floor. "I was fine until I got tackled by a dryad." When she tried to pull away with an indignant huff, I hugged her tight for another moment. "I'm so glad you were out of that whole mess."

She stepped back as a disembodied voice said, "We ... are ... pleased ... you ... sustained ... no ... lasting ... harm ... Mister ... Mann."

My eyes widened as I glanced around. "Uh, voice synthesizer upgrade?"

Eleri wrinkled her nose. "Yeah. Hector's working on the speed and inflection, but at least Miss Pennybaker doesn't have to type everything now."

"That's, um, great."

"She might come to our next book club meeting."

"Really?" I tugged at the neck of my henley. It was clear Eleri had really bonded with Miss Pennybaker. I hoped she wouldn't be devastated if Yannick escorted our resident Victorian Suffragette onward. "I'm thinking you should branch out into movies. You know, *Cabin in the Woods. Winnie the Pooh and the Honey Tree. The Petrified Forest.*"

She stuck her tongue out at me. "Don't be snarky, Hugh. Our club makes a *difference.* We're *activists,* which Miss Pennybaker *totally* gets. Plus, she has a ton of experience with civil disobedience." She grinned. "It'll be fun."

"If you say so."

"We ... do ... Mister ... Mann."

I started to lower myself into a chair, but Eleri said, "Don't sit down. There are some people here to see you."

I groaned, but it was probably better that I remained standing. If I sat, I might not be able to get up again. "Let me guess. Paimon?"

She grinned. "Yep. He's waiting in the staff room."

"Terrorizing the untethered souls? Or has Yannick finally done his duty by them?"

"Not yet." She resumed her place behind the desk. "He's sulking upstairs in the Little Conference Room. Herne's with him, although"—she smiled slyly—"Herne has requested that you put them first on your agenda since he has a *date.*"

I chuckled. "They're right up near the top." I turned to head for my office.

"That's not all."

I glanced over my shoulder. "Lachlan's not here, is he?"

"Nope." She tilted the chair back on its gimbals. "But a pod of selkies showed up. I put them in the fourth floor conference room." She held her arms out wide. "The big one."

I grimaced. "There are that many of them?"

"Yep. And they *really* want to see you." She smirked. "Your Highness."

"Shut up," I muttered. "Could you let Herne know I'll be with him as soon as I can?"

"I ... will ... inform ... him."

"Uh, thanks, Miss Pennybaker." I high-tailed it out of the lobby and hurried up to my third floor office.

Since Paimon wanted *all* of his shots, I queued up fifty copies each and sent them to the super-speedy-high-res photo printer with a magically unending paper supply that Zeke had installed for us practically the minute he started at Quest. If Paimon needed more than that, he could damn well wait for them.

I collected them from the collator—also magically expanding—loaded them into an empty box and headed up to the staff room. Paimon was kicked back, his cloven hooves propped on the table, ankles crossed. His arms were extended to either side of him. A nail buffer danced over the claws on his left hand and a glass of amber liquid—probably bourbon, given the bottle marching through the air to the credenza—floated into his right.

"Ah, Hugh! So happy to see you up and about." His gaze landed on the box and he grinned. "Oooohhh." He dropped his feet to the floor. "Have you brought me something?"

"Your photos. Fifty copies of each."

He pouted. "Only fifty?"

"If you want more, you can order them, but this is what I've got for now."

He set his bourbon on the table, waved his invisible manicurist away, and sauntered over, selecting the top photo from the box. "Stunning. But then, it's me, so it couldn't be anything less." He laid it lovingly back in the box. "What do I owe you?"

I blinked. I had sort of assumed that I'd been doing this pro bono. Collecting political capital for Quest with Sheol upper management. Plus, he'd vanquished Athaniel, albeit a little late. "Well—"

"Yes, yes, I know I exceeded the scope of the original agreement, but your work was so outstanding that I simply couldn't resist. So naturally I expect your remuneration to reflect that. You needn't feel any reticence to demand precisely what they're worth."

I narrowed my eyes at him. Was this a trick? That word—*precisely*—seemed like it might be the gateway to some seriously unfortunate negotiations. But Paimon, as vain and self-centered as he was, had never been anything but straightforward—at least with me.

So I looked him in the eye and told him my price.

CHAPTER
TWENTY-FOUR

After I left Paimon, I made a quick call before heading to the fourth floor conference room. As soon as I walked in, every selkie in the place—and there were *a lot* of them—rose to their feet. Calum and his lousy broom were front and center as they all intoned, "Your Highness."

I glared at them. "Enough of that."

"But, Your Highness," Calum said, "as consort to our king, we owe you our deepest respect, including addressing you by your proper title."

"If I'm due such dang respect"—they flinched a little at my tone—"then what gives with the shotgun wedding?"

Calum exchange mystified glances with several other selkies. "Shotgun? We deal not with firearms."

"Virtual shotgun, then. You forced Lachlan and me into a marriage that neither one of us consented to."

"But...but His Majesty said—"

"That's another thing. He doesn't want to be king. He's told you that dozens, if not hundreds, of times. Why do you keep hounding him?"

"Because we need him to stand for us. To protect us."

"Protect you from what?"

His expression turned shifty. "From...those who would exploit us."

"You mean humans?" I asked dryly.

He held up one hand, palm out. "Not you, of course! We know your connection to His Majesty is just and true. But from others who are not so…righteous."

"Then why in blazes don't you protect *each other*?"

His bushy white brows drew together. "I don't understand."

I paced the width of the room. "From all the lore I've read, selkies suffered most often when some asshole fisherman caught one of you alone. Set up a buddy system, for Pete's sake." I flung my arms out. "This isn't the Middle Ages. There are technological solutions to help keep you safe." I jabbed a finger at Calum. "In fact, I know a werewolf who would probably love to tackle that problem."

"But…but what about protecting our interests with other supes?"

"Ever hear of collective bargaining agreements?" They all shook their heads simultaneously, because of course they did. Lachlan had warned me that they were looking for somebody else to shoulder the work. Well, that ended here. "You should check in with the dryad at the desk downstairs for details on alternate management structures, because if you'd stop stalking Lachlan and ambushing people with random weddings, you could probably accomplish a lot by working *together*."

"It was nae random," Calum said indignantly. "His Majesty is enamored of you and you of him." He tapped his chest over his *calon*. "It is clear for all to see, awaiting only the—"

"That's enough." I ran my hands through my hair, heaving a sigh. "Look, regardless of how Lachlan and I feel or don't feel about one another, it's nobody's business but ours."

His expression turned sly. "Nay. 'Tis our business now. He is our king and you his consort."

"Nope. Lachlan and I will figure out what this unexpected marriage means"—another finger jab—"*on our own*, but he's not your king anymore and I've got nothing to do with any of you whatsoever, and never have."

Calum drew himself up, triumph all over his face. "He accepted our tribute. He is our king, whether he protest or no."

"Guess again." I pulled a ruby the size of my fist out of my jacket pocket—the ruby Lachlan had handed over to Paimon as unnecessary payment to rescue me in Sheol. Paimon had returned it to me just now in payment for his photos—and seemed surprised that I had asked for so little. I slapped the ruby into Calum's hand. "There you go. Tribute refunded in full. Now, I've got something important to do, so..." I strode to the door and flung it open, revealing Frang—or at least everything but his head, which extended above the door frame. *Perfect timing.* He'd answered my call with no questions asked. "Frang will escort you through Faerie to wherever you choose to go—as long as it's not Lachlan's boat." Their mouths gaped like a school of herring, and I grinned. "Don't forget to tip him, or he might get a tad cranky."

I gave Frang a fist bump on my way out the door. "Next stop," I muttered, "Slacker Death."

When I got to the Little Conference Room, Yannick was huddled in a chair, staring sullenly at the table top. Herne was at the window, his back to the room.

"Sorry to keep you waiting," I said brightly.

"Shall ... I ... bring ... refreshments?"

I blinked at...nothing. "Ah, no, Miss Pennybaker. This shouldn't take long. Thank you, though."

"I ... shall ... remain ... in ... case ... circumstances ... alter."

"Sure. Great. Thanks." I speared Yannick with a glare. "In fact, Mr. Tan here might need to dictate a letter dropping the lawsuit against me. Isn't that right?"

Yannick shrugged. "Whatever. Although nothing's changed. There are still way too many souls wanting a piece of me. I can't even *think*, let alone send any of them on."

"Young ... man. Stop ... whining."

His jaw dropped as he stared at a spot directly across from him. *Oh, right.* He could see the untethered souls. If he couldn't, he wouldn't be able to do his job.

Not that he was doing it now.

"I'm not whi—"

"You ... are. There ... is ... nothing ... amiss ... that ... a ... little ... organization ... and ... discipline ... will ... not ... solve."

"Yeah, well, that's something I apparently don't have," Yannick muttered with a fulminating glance my way.

"Perhaps ... not." A pause. "Most ... assuredly ... not. However ... I ... most ... assuredly ... do."

He eyed her warily as Herne joined me by the door—and I could swear that I could *almost* see her outline. "I don't suppose *you* want to move on. 'Cause I could definitely do that. Like now."

"I ... shall ... not ... depart ... until ... my ... cause ... is ... won ... and ... all ... women ... everywhere ... are ... granted ... equal ... rights."

"In other words," I murmured to Herne, "she'll be around forever."

"I ... shall ... prepare ... a ... roster ... for ... you ... each ... day ... and ... you ... will ... report ... here ... for ... your ... assignments." A notepad and pen floated over to the table and a chair swiveled to accept its invisible occupant. "Let ... us ... begin."

"You know, I feel a little bad about that," I said to Herne as I shut the door on Yannick and Miss Pennybaker. "It's like being stranded with your strict Great Aunt Ethel for eternity."

Herne's chuckle rumbled from deep in his chest and my eyebrows shot up. He wasn't exactly the cheeriest guy around. In fact, I don't think I'd ever heard him laugh before. "I expect it will not be as dire as that. And at any rate, he'll no longer be alone. That will count for something." His voice turned soft at his last words.

"Things going well with Wyn, then?"

He nodded, although I noticed he was careful to keep his antlers clear of my head. "Very well, indeed. He is awaiting me now." An expression of mingled joy and bewilderment suffused his face. "He says he will always wait for me, and welcome me on my return."

Do you know what it's like to watch a meta-god blush? No? Then let me tell you: It's freaking awesome.

"That's fantastic, Herne. I'm really happy for you." I held out my hand, and after he gazed at it, perplexed, for a moment, he shook it. "And thank you for your help with this whole mess."

His expression darkened to the one I was accustomed to seeing on his face. "Much of the blame fell to me. If I had not—"

"Nope." I held up my hands, palms out. "Not hearing that. You did your part. Yannick dropped the ball. Or perhaps the supe council and the combined management of Sheol and Elysium dropped the ball when they didn't dismantle Athaniel's matrix back when he first tried to frame Zeke. If they'd done their jobs then, Athaniel would never have been able to catfish you in an attempt to regain his former status— which, by the way, was *never* happening. So you've got nothing to blame yourself for."

"I thank you, Hugh. In addition to rescuing me from my own folly, you have been an enduring champion to me and...mine." Another blush. "You may always call upon me at any time."

I gazed up at him, my eyes narrowing as an idea occurred to me. "You know, there *is* something else you could do for me."

"You have only to name it, and it is yours."

CHAPTER
TWENTY-FIVE

I was gazing through the window at the depths of Loch Ness when Lachlan appeared at my shoulder.

"Matthew."

I shivered, as I always did at the way my name sounded in Lachlan's swoony Scottish accent. "Look." I jerked my chin at the window. "Nessie's got a friend."

Lachlan peered past the plaid curtains at the two sea serpents dancing in the water. His eyebrows shot up. "Methinks that's more than a friend."

I jerked my gaze away from his jawline—not an easy task—and peered out at Nessie and her companion. Who were twined together in a *very* suggestive fashion. "Is that— Are they—"

Lachlan chuckled and twitched the curtains over the glass. "Perhaps we should give them some privacy."

"Right. Privacy." *Privacy* was the reason I'd asked Herne to transport me back to the cottage under the loch, why I'd asked him to collect Lachlan from my place and bring him here too. This seemed like one of the only places we could be ensured of not being interrupted.

Although...we'd barged in on Wyn when he was staying here, so I suppose there was still a slim chance. But it would take a concerted effort, so this was probably the best I could ever hope for.

I took Lachlan's hand. "Sit down with me?" He raised his eyebrows—probably because he expected me to either lead him straight for the bedroom or else tell him to never darken my door again. However, he allowed me to draw him down next to me on the plaid sofa. I glanced down at his hand, at the wedding band gleaming on his finger. At my hand, still bare. "We should talk about some things."

He sighed. "Matthew. I hope you know I would never force you into a relationship before you were ready. The selkies should never have put you in this position."

I tilted my head. "They put you in the same position."

"Aye." His lips curved in a soft smile. "But since it's exactly where I wished to be, I cannot complain."

"Not even about the kingship?"

His smile faded. "I made that bed myself. There's naught to do but lie in it."

"Not so fast, bucko." I tapped his cheek. "You're not lying in any bed unless it's one that I'm in, too."

Hope flared to life in his dark eyes, but then his shoulders fell. "But our joining will always be shadowed by my duties."

"Not anymore." I grinned at him. "You're off the hook. As it were."

He scowled. *Ah, there he was. My Lachlan.* "I don't understand. I accepted their tribute."

I did my best impression of a warning buzzer. "Wrong. Their tribute is right back where it started—in their sneaky little hands."

"But…how?"

I grinned. "For my very valuable photography services, I charged Paimon precisely one ruby. One *specific* ruby, which I then returned to Calum. I'd say I returned it with my compliments, but I wasn't very complimentary."

A smile lit his face, and he grabbed me in a hug that nearly crushed the breath out of me. "*Mo cridhe*, you are without a doubt the most extraordinary man in all the realms."

"I wouldn't say that," I wheezed. "And I won't be able to say anything unless you ease up on the death grip."

He released me at once and almost leaped across the sofa from me. "I'm sorry. I know you don't want me."

I goggled at him. "Excuse me, Lachlan, but WTF? I've been trying to jump your bones practically since we met. We've finally cleared all the obstacles in our way. Why on earth—or anywhere else, for that matter—would you think I don't want you?"

His brows knitted in confusion. "Because you won't swim with me."

I threw up my hands. "There you go with that swim thing again. I know that couples are supposed to do things with each other outside the bedroom, but we'll have few enough years together as it is. Do we really have to spend some of it with me bobbing like an ice cube in the Pacific?"

"But..." His confusion seemed to increase. "You know why I want to swim with you."

"Other than to see how far into my body my junk retreats from the cold? No. I haven't a clue."

"I explained this to you." His forehead wrinkled as though he were searching his memory, but he didn't break out the scowl. "I'm sure I did. When you worried so about how quickly you'd age, how short our time would be. Didn't I?"

"Didn't you what?"

"Tell you that a swim is not just a swim, not when a selkie takes his mate on his back, both of their skins embraced by the sea."

I squinted at him. "Okay. I'll bite. If it's not a swim, what is it?"

He cupped my face in both his hands. "It is a mating dance, *mo cridhe*, much as Nessie and her swain are doing outside at this moment. When a selkie swims with his human mate, his mate is joined to him, heart to heart. And more."

I frowned at him. "If you're talking about seal sex, I'm not onboard with that. At all."

Lachlan threw back his head and laughed, the jerk. "No seal sex, *mo cridhe*, never fear. It means as long as we swim together, you share my *calon*."

I blinked at him. "Say what now?"

"How cruel would it have been for the old gods to form humans as our perfect mates, yet prevent us from biding with them? True selkie mates, those who—"

"Are foolish enough to dunk themselves in the ocean?"

"Those who engage in the mating swim at least once each year, share the selkie's *calon*."

My jaw sagged. "You mean I'm a supe?"

He kissed me gently. "No, *mo cridhe*. You are human still, god-touched or no. But we share a life now. I will age more quickly. You will age more slowly. It is a true sharing."

"B-but...I'm *draining your life*?" I pulled away. "No. Absolutely not. It ain't happening."

"You are not draining me. We are *sharing*. Our lifespans will still far exceed an ordinary human's, but we will live them together." He peered at me, his eyes full of concern. "But I will understand if you are still angry about Calum's trick with the besom and don't wish to—"

I jumped on him then, sending him toppling back onto the cushions with me sprawled on top of him. "Are you kidding?" I kissed him, not in the least gently. "Of course I want to. Although..." I lifted one eyebrow. "Technically, you still haven't *asked* me."

He grinned, his lips still shiny from our kiss, and sat up. He set me aside, much to my dismay, because *holy crap*. We would age *together*. For a *long freaking time*. He reached behind his neck and untied a leather thong I hadn't noticed before. He lifted it from beneath his henley, and a gold band, the same as his, glinted in the light.

"Matthew, *mo cridhe*, would you do me the very great honor of being my friend, my mate, my husband, for as long as we dwell together?" I nodded as he held the ring over my left hand. "If you agree," he whispered, "you must say, *I promise by the heart of the sea.*"

"I promise…" I had to clear a throat gone tight and thick. "I promise by the heart of the sea."

"As I pledge myself to you, by the heart of the sea."

He slid the ring on and lifted my hand to kiss where it nestled on my finger, a perfect fit—both the ring and his lips, in case you were wondering.

I threaded my other hand through his hair and brought his mouth to mine in a kiss that started out gentle and sweet, but transitioned to hungry and dirty. "Lachlan," I gasped.

"Yes, husband?"

"There's a bed right through that door, and I've waited way too long to feel you on me and in me. Can we *please*—"

"Of course, *mo cridhe*. I too have waited too long for this."

I kissed him again. "And then afterwards"—another kiss or maybe seven—"although not *too* soon after, since we're here until Herne collects us tomorrow morning—" I got distracted by Lachlan's lips against my throat. "Nnnng."

"Afterwards, what, Matthew?"

"Afterwards…" I cupped his face in both hands and kissed him again. "Afterwards? Let's go for a swim."

WHAT'S NEXT?
Check out the new mythmatched romance!

the skinny on
Djinni

Being in tech time-out totally sucks.

Hector Gonzales knew the danger when he hacked the magic grid to marry it with human technology. He'd never imagined *this* system crash: A total tech suspension while the tradition-bound supe council reviews his case. He's reduced to running errands for his friends, and seriously? How had people survived before GPS? Then several wrong turns—thank you so much, stupid paper map—lead him to a remote burger joint. And when he spots the cute guy behind the counter? His wolf wakes up and howls *You have arrived at your destination.*

Getting fired—again—totally sucks.

Rafi Abbas tries to give customers what they want, he really does. However, when he gets distracted by the lovely man with the gorgeous brown skin, he screws up another customer's order and his boss fires him on the spot. With no money, no job, and soon nowhere to live, Rafi has no business saying yes when the lovely man asks him out. But something about Hector whispers *home.*

Obeying the Secrecy Pact totally sucks.

To keep the supe community safe, werewolves cannot partner romantically with humans. That rule has been programmed into Hector since he was a pup. But as the day slides from bad to worse to are-you-freaking-kidding-me, Hector sees the moratorium for what it is: ridiculous and outdated. For Rafi, he's willing to challenge the status quo.

After all, things can't very well get worse than worst. Right?

The Skinny on Djinni is a M/M paranormal romance set in E.J. Russell's popular Mythmatched story universe. While it features instinctual attraction, fated mates are *not* a thing. You'll recognize some familiar faces from other Mythmatched tales, and although the romance—complete with HEA—stands alone, the story answers a couple of long-standing questions!

the skinny on
Djinni

The road was so narrow that it took Hector three attempts to turn the truck around. He rolled down his window, just a crack, enough to let in the scents of the woods. But not more than that, because it was freaking *cold* in January. The scents changed as he reached the outskirts of Everhall, with a trace of ocean salt mixing with the heady forest smells.

He cast a longing glance at Getchur Burgers as he passed. Could he stop in and get the counter guy's name? Maybe he was an online gamer. They could connect—

Nope. They couldn't. Because Hector wouldn't be online for the foreseeable future. Maybe once he was back on his tech feet, so to speak, and with more than twenty dollars in his pocket, he could come back and ask the guy out for coffee or lunch or something. Hector wasn't like Dakota, who could cheerfully flit from one hookup to the next without bothering to learn more than a first name and favorite sex position; or Jordan, who was content—it seemed—to pine from afar over a series of buff, unattainable men.

When faced with a programming question, Hector liked to immerse himself in the challenge, exploring the possibilities until he lit on the perfect, elegant solution. He wanted to immerse himself in a relationship the same way.

Or at least he did now. He'd never been tempted before. Maybe he was a late bloomer, like his Tio Fernando, who'd stayed single most of his life until he'd met Leo at a clan gathering and proposed before the closing feast. When Tio Fernando had declared his intention to transfer from their

Umatilla pack all the way to Klamath to join Leo's pack, their alpha had asked testily why he'd made such a hasty decision. Tio had replied, "When you know, you know."

Hector got what Tio meant now. He wanted to *immerse* himself and learn everything about Cute Burger Guy. What did he like to do? Was he into video games? What were his favorite foods? Hector had a feeling that even if CBG liked pineapple on his pizza, Hector would find a way to forgive him.

The sex stuff? Yeah, maybe he could get into that, but that would come later. Maybe never, if the only thing CBG was interested in was friendship, and that would be okay. But there was *something* there. Hector just knew it, from the way their eyes had locked over the cash register. The way CBG kept glancing at him while he filled that big jerk's order. Hector groaned. *The way he saw me make a fool of myself and whack my head on the table.*

He rubbed the back of his head. It still twinged a little, which was probably a good thing. It would remind him not to be such a dork the next time. Cool. Smooth. Sophisticated. Yeah, he could be cool, like Mal Kendrick, his fae self-defense teacher. Smooth, like Chase, his old Howling RA. Sophisticated, like Quentin Bertrand-Harrington, Boston blue-blood incubus.

In a pig shifter's eye.

Hector sighed. Well, maybe CBG was into awkward geeky guys. He'd heard that some people were, although he'd never met one. But there was no point borrowing trouble now because he couldn't even ask for a coffee date until this whole tech suspension was over and his sentence handed down.

So, with one final glance at Getchur Burgers in the side mirror, he turned down the road that ought to lead to the estate agent's location. The residential area in Everhall was smaller than Dewton's, and considerably less scenic. The houses closest to the main business street looked like they'd been fabricated out of leftovers from 1960s tract homes, but further along the road, they seemed to get more attractive. Larger, on bigger lots, and— *Hold on.*

A figure in a navy peacoat, shoulders slumped and head bowed, a battered pack on his back, was trudging along the side of the road. Even without the red and white visor dangling from his hand, Hector recognized him. Those black curls were a dead giveaway.

CBG.

Hector's middle did a loop-the-loop. Could he score that coffee date now? CBG was clearly done with work, and Hector still had thirteen dollars and change. Why not start a better acquaintance today? *I'll just pull up alongside him and say hi.* That wouldn't look too serial-killer-freaky, would it? He winced. Yeah, probably it would, although at least he was driving a pickup with an open bed and not some creepy panel van.

He flexed his hands on the steering wheel. Maybe this wasn't such a great idea. He was already late meeting the estate agent, thanks to getting his directions upside down. And there was the whole matter of him being on probation pending trial. Yeah, quite the catch.

Oh, and CBG was human, so there was that. While some supe species were allowed to form committed relationships with humans, werewolves were not among them. Better if Hector just kept going. He could always come back later once his life had settled down again. After all, there weren't any rules about having human *friends*—mostly—as long as the friendship was terminated before the human noticed that their *friend* wasn't aging in the ordinary way.

But as Hector drove past at a bare creep, he couldn't resist a glance in the side-view mirror, and when he caught the expression on CBG's face— *Remus's balls.* The poor guy looked completely *wrecked.* Had that asshole made trouble for him?

Hector's wolf growled—which translated into a rumbling in Hector's chest that he'd never felt before: His wolf was *pissed* that CBG was upset.

He stomped the clutch and jammed on the brakes. He hadn't been going more than ten mph, so his tires didn't screech on the pavement, but the sudden stop made CBG look up, alarm chasing over his thin, high-cheek-boned face.

Hector grinned, hoping it didn't look killer-clown disturbing, and waved through the rear window. Then he turned off the truck and unbuckled his seatbelt. He had to scoot across the bench seat to roll down the passenger side window, since vintage trucks didn't have automatic anything—which was probably why the council hadn't objected to Ted loaning it to him.

He leaned out the window. "Hey. Hi. I, um, remember me? I'm the dork—"

"Of course." CBG smiled tentatively. "Hector, right?"

Hector blinked. "You remember my name?" He smacked his forehead. "You probably remember everybody's name, since that's kind of your job. To work with people. And it wasn't that long ago, so I shouldn't be surprised."

"I don't remember everyone. But I remember you."

Hector brightened. "Yeah?"

"Yeah." CBG's smile faded and he turned away. "I'm sorry you had to see all that."

Hector's wolf scrabbled to get out, not to bite and rend, but to cuddle and comfort. *Down, boy. What is* wrong *with you?* "That asshole guy? You probably have to deal with jerks like that all the time, huh? I couldn't do it. I'm, um, not great at peopling." He winced. "In case you can't tell by my total lack of game here."

CBG peeked at him from under his tumbled curls. "Game?"

Hector snorted. "Pretty pathetic, right? I can whoop any of my packm— pals' butts on Nintendo or PlayStation, but talking to a cute guy? I've got nothing."

The smile glimmered again, revealing an unexpected dimple in one lean cheek. "You think I'm cute?"

"Well, yeah. *Obviously*." Hector grimaced. "But I'm, you know, me, so I don't expect—"

"Ithinkyou'recutetoo," CBG blurted.

Hector hadn't known his wolf could *purr*. "Really? That's great. That's really— Hey, would you like to grab a cup of coffee or tea or a soda with me now? If you've got time. I mean, it looks like you're done with work for the day, but you might have other plans."

The dimple vanished. "I've got no plans whatsoever. And I'm done with Getchur Burgers for good." He dropped his gaze, suddenly very interested in toeing a pebble aside with his faded red sneaker. "I just got fired."

"What?" Hector's chest constricted. "Was it because of me? Did I do something to—"

CBG held up both hands and frowned at the visor as though he'd forgotten he was holding it. "Totally not you, I promise."

"That asshole then?" A growl struggled to get out, but Hector suppressed it. Barely. "If he—"

"No, no." CBG heaved a sigh. "It was all me. Not for the first time, either." His face twisted in a lopsided smile. "In fact, this is a milestone: The number of times I've been fired now exceeds the number of years I've been alive." He sighed again. "It could be a record."

"In that case, I think we should definitely grab a drink somewhere." Hector bit his lip, shifting a little on the seat. "That is, if you want to?"

CBG met Hector's gaze, and *Remus*, but his eyes were pretty. Darker than midnight and fringed with really long lashes, which Hector had never realized were a *thing* for him. "I'd like that. Thank you."

Another purr from his wolf—and Hector was *never* admitting that to his friends because they wouldn't let him live it down. "Awesome. But first"—he cleared his throat—"could you tell me your name? I've just been thinking of you as CBG and I know that's not right."

"CBG?"

"Cute Burger Guy."

His eyes lit up, crinkling at the edges, and he chuckled, a warm burr that went straight to Hector's middle. "My name is Rafi Ab—"

Wham.

A MESSAGE FROM
E.J.

Dear Reader,

Thank you so much for reading *Death on Denial*, the fourth book in my Quest Investigations mystery series! If you're curious about Matt's backstory, you might want to check out his debut on the Mythmatched stage in *Single White Incubus*, the first in the Supernatural Selection trilogy about a paranormal matchmaking agency, or his later appearance (along with Jordan's introduction) in *Howling on Hold*. If you'd like to go all the way back to the Mythmatched beginnings, the story world dawned with *Cutie and the Beast*, a paranormal rom-com where a cursed fae warrior turned psychologist clashes with his determined temporary office manager. As you might expect, hijinks ensue!

You can see all my books on my website, https://ejrussell.com, or on my Amazon author page here: https://www.amazon.com/author/ej_russell. Most are also available at Apple, Kobo, and Barnes and Noble.

Would you like exclusive content and ARC giveaways, not to mention gratuitous dance videos? Then I'd love for you to join me in Reality Optional, my Facebook fan group (https://facebook.com/groups/reality.optional). My newsletter is the place to get the latest dish on new releases, sales, and more. I promise I only send one out when I've got...well...news. You can subscribe here: https://ejrussell.com/newsletter.

All my best,
—E

ALSO BY
E.J. RUSSELL

Paranormal Romance
Mythmatched Universe
Fae Out of Water Trilogy
Cutie and the Beast
The Druid Next Door
Bad Boy's Bard

Supernatural Selection Trilogy
Single White Incubus
Vampire With Benefits
Demon on the Down-Low

Other Mythmatched Romances
Howling on Hold
Possession in Session
Witch Under Wraps
Cursed is the Worst
The Skinny on Djinni
Assassin by Accident (part of Carnival of Mysteries)

Mythmatched Companion Stories
Rusty's Really Bad Day (free to newsletter subscribers)
Second First Date (free to newsletter subscribers)

Quest Investigations Mysteries
Five Dead Herrings
The Hound of the Burgervilles

The Lady Under the Lake
Death on Denial

Art Medium Series
The Artist's Touch
Tested in Fire
Art Medium: The Complete Collection (omnibus edition)

Legend Tripping Series
Stumptown Spirits
Wolf's Clothing

Enchanted Occasions Series
Best Beast
Nudging Fate
Devouring Flame

Royal Powers Series (shared world)
Duking It Out
Duke the Hall
King's Ex

Magic Emporium Series (shared world)
Purgatory Playhouse

Monster Till Midnight

Historical Romance
Silent Sin

Contemporary Romance
Camera Shy
The Thomas Flair
Mystic Man

For a Good Time, Call... (A Bluewater Bay novel, with Anne Tenino)

Holiday Shorts (separately)
The Probability of Mistletoe
An Everyday Hero
A Swants Soiree
or all three together in
Christmas Kisses

Geeklandia Series
The Boyfriend Algorithm (M/F)
Clickbait

Writing as Nelle Heran
(traditional cozy mystery)

Crafty Sleuth Series (with C.K. Eastland)
Die Cut
Mixed Media
Found Objects (*coming soon*)

ABOUT THE
AUTHOR

E.J. Russell (she/her), author of the award-winning Mythmatched paranormal romance series, writes LGBTQ+ romance and mystery in a rainbow of flavors. Count on high snark, low angst, and happy endings.

Reality? Eh, not so much.

She's married to Curmudgeonly Husband, a man who cares even less about sports than she does. Luckily, C.H. also loves to cook, or all three of their children (Lovely Daughter and Darling Sons A and B) would have survived on nothing but Cheerios, beef jerky, and Satsuma mandarins (the extent of E.J.'s culinary skill set).

E.J. also writes traditional cozy mystery as Nelle Heran. She lives in rural Oregon, enjoys visits from her wonderful adult children, and indulges in good books, red wine, and the occasional hyperbole.

News & Social Media:
Website: https://ejrussell.com
Newsletter: https://ejrussell.com/newsletter

ACKNOWLEDGEMENTS

Many thanks to my awesome beta readers—Kelly Jensen, Lisa Leoni-Kinley, and lyric apted—for suggestions, advice, and encouragement; to Meg DesCamp, Queen of Puns, for editing magic; to L.C. Chase for the adorable cover; to my family for endless support; and of course to you, my readers, for accompanying me on this wild journey.

Without all of you, I wouldn't be able to continue to do what I love.